Praise for *Why I Love Horror*

"Spratford, well-known in the library world as a horror expert, has gathered the most important voices in the genre today . . . The results are illuminating, moving, and inspiring."

—*Booklist*, starred review

"A wonderful autopsy of both the horror genre and the current batch of hell-scribblers and fear-junkies who are guiding it."

—Chuck Wendig, bestselling author of *The Book of Accidents*

"One of the genre's true tastemakers, Becky Spratford has gathered in this book of essays the perfect rogues' gallery to address the question all horror lovers are asked—'Why horror?' Horror's top stars and brightest lights dig into the question with passion, insight, and profound empathy, all of which are genre hallmarks perhaps even more vital than terror, evil, and gore."

—Christopher Golden, *New York Times* bestselling author of
Road of Bones and *The House of Last Resort*

"The essays collected here are probing, insightful, and deeply intimate. There's a quivering, bloody heart rooted at the center of this book and shared by all those who partake in the sacred communion of fear. A truly remarkable achievement."

—Eric LaRocca, author of
Things Have Gotten Worse Since We Last Spoke

"A joyfully effusive love letter to the genre. If you've ever needed a reason to dip your toes into horror or wondered why it has so many aficionados, this beautifully curated book presents a multiplicity of reasons."

—Cassandra Khaw, author of *Nothing But Blackened Teeth*

"You can call this book a 'love letter' because of the powerful affection thrumming through it, but rarely has a love letter also been so instructive and insightful. To borrow a phrase from Becky Spratford herself, this book is a must-own for all libraries—and that includes personal ones."

—Nat Cassidy, author of *When the Wolf Comes Home* and *Mary*

Why I Love Horror

Essays on Horror Literature

Edited by
Becky Siegel Spratford

SAGA S PRESS

LONDON   **NEW YORK**   TORONTO
AMSTERDAM/ANTWERP   NEW DELHI   SYDNEY/MELBOURNE

SAGA PRESS
AN IMPRINT OF SIMON & SCHUSTER, LLC

1230 AVENUE OF THE AMERICAS, NEW YORK, NEW YORK 10020

Compilation copyright © 2025 by Becky Siegel Spratford
See page 256 for additional copyright information.

First Saga Press trade paperback edition September 2025

SAGA PRESS and colophon are trademarks of Simon & Schuster, LLC

Simon & Schuster strongly believes in freedom of expression and stands against censorship in all its forms. For more information, visit BooksBelong.com.

For information about special discounts for bulk purchases, please contact Simon & Schuster Special Sales at 1-866-506-1949 or business@simonandschuster.com.

The Simon & Schuster Speakers Bureau can bring authors to your live event. For more information or to book an event, contact the Simon & Schuster Speakers Bureau at 1-866-248-3049 or visit our website at www.simonspeakers.com.

Interior design by Kathryn A. Kenney-Peterson

Manufactured in the United States of America

3   5   7   9   10   8   6   4   2

Library of Congress Control Number: 2025939769

ISBN 978-1-6682-0509-9
ISBN 978-1-6682-0510-5 (ebook)

For the Halloween Library League:
Emily, Konrad, Lila, and Yaika

Contents

Introduction

Welcome, fellow readers of the dark and deliciously disturbing.

Horror isn't just a genre, it's a calling. A secret handshake in the dark. You made a deal at some point to embark on a journey few are brave enough to accept. You have arrived at this way station at the precise moment in time determined by this calling. You have traveled down a twisting, treacherous path, all its dangers and pitfalls known only to you. You have mapped your way through shadowy hallways, haunted forests, and menacing alleyways. You enjoyed walking through graveyards, picking your way through the tombstones with only a flashlight to light the way. You jumped at the chance to explore haunted houses, ghostly shipwrecks, and uncharted waters. All these adventures, experienced in the palm of your hand, escalating with every turn of the page. And now you're here.

Welcome to this gathering of voices—a kaleidoscope of perspectives from some of the finest writers in the realm of horror. A collection of essays penned by masters of the macabre, revealing their unique path that has led them here, to this way station; a place designed for you to rest from the calling of your stack of unread horror books and enjoy this time of refreshment and unity.

These authors, whose imaginations have spawned tales that haunt and thrill, offer you a glimpse into their deeply personal journey with horror. They have been summoned to give an account by the horror librarian Becky Siegel Spratford, the genre's most capable and steadfast champion—and my mentor.

This is where I get to brag about my friend. When I first started reviewing horror for various platforms, Becky saw me and took me under her wing; she wasn't the first librarian to notice my enthusiasm for reading but definitely the one who has poured the most into me. In the tradition of all superheroes who don't wear capes who have gone before her, Becky advocates for the underdog genre, horror. I don't know what horror did to deserve such a mighty voice (this book will surely tell you), but we got her, and she works tirelessly day in and day out to shine a bright light on these dark books. It's because of her example I learned how to put the right book in the right reader's hands.

Allow me to introduce myself. I'm Sadie Hartmann, but you might know me better as Mother Horror on social media. I am the author of the Bram Stoker Award–winning guide *101 Horror Books to Read Before You're Murdered* and the newly released *Feral and Hysterical: Mother Horror's Ultimate Reading Guide to Dark and Disturbing Fiction by Women*.

At the beginning of my individual genre adventure, I was a gawky, insecure, scrawny girl with a funky sense of style and ratty, unbrushed hair. A loner maybe seen with a few friends from time to time, but basically, I was what was commonly known as a "geek" or "dork." An outsider who felt safer eating her lunch in the classroom, reading books, than outside on the playground.

Nobody would know by looking at me (in my mismatched, out-of-date clothes, on my hot-pink Barbie bike with a banana seat and plastic tassels on the handlebars) that I had great taste in music and even better taste in horror books. But one day they would.

Horror has always felt like the language my soul speaks when no one else is listening. Horror understands what it means to carry fear in your bones—not as something to be embarrassed about, but as something that shapes you into who you really are. For someone timid, for someone who knows the weight of fear day in and day out, horror offers an unexpected refuge. It's a space where fear isn't a failing or something to overcome, but a tool to unlock pieces of myself I've hidden away. Fear is the essential ingredient for a whole genre of books. It's acknowledged, honored, and even celebrated. Horror takes all my restless anxieties—the ones that simmer just beneath the surface—and gives them form. It allows me to face them on my terms, in the safety of a story. Horror is empowering for someone like me. I can step into the fire willingly, feeling the heat, the danger, but knowing that it's contained. A story can push me to the brink and pull me back. I witness characters enduring horrors far worse than my own struggles and trials.

If they can do this, so can you.

I think I love it because horror doesn't flinch. It doesn't lie or sugar-coat or wrap the world in pretty packaging. It acknowledges the cracks in the veneer. It holds up a mirror to expose the messy, vulnerable parts we'd rather ignore. And in that, I've always felt seen. But a love of horror can also be shared.

Long before words on paper, our ancestors shared stories and songs by firelight, warning of prowling beasts, restless spirits, and the terrors that lie just beyond the circle of light. Horror has always been a way to name the unnamable and confront the things that frighten us together, as a community. I love to imagine what the world's first horror story was about and how it might have been told. The wild hand gestures and eyes with all the white showing. The people who heard the story went back to where they laid their heads at night and thought about the horrors they heard. They barely slept a wink that night, and they woke up and couldn't wait to tell someone about the nightmares threatening their peace of mind. I love that sometimes horror demands to be shared. It's a wild and untamed thing that grows restless if we bottle it up and keep it inside. It threatens to come spilling out of our mouths. Our bodies betray us with our hairs standing on end or our jaws dropped open or our hands shaking. We must tell.

For me, a compulsion to absorb horror, but for others, a compulsion to create. For some, writing is an act of catharsis to process personal fears and traumas. For others, it is an artistic rebellion, a means to disrupt comfort and challenge societal norms. In these essays, you will find confessions of childhood terrors, reflections on the nature of fear, and explorations of the dark beauty that horror holds. You will also see how diverse this genre can be.

You will see yourself in these horror origin stories.

As you turn the pages, I invite you to meet these authors for the first time as they step out from behind their fictional stories to offer you their own story. Where they have been and how they got here.

Each essay is introduced with a brief note from Becky, offering context and a nudge toward some of the authors' works you might explore afterward. You'll also witness Becky's greatest gift, her ability to connect readers with read-alikes and comps: *If you like that author's work, consider reading this author.* It's a special skill honed over many years of reading, reviewing, and advocating horror. It's her wheelhouse, her craft.

She is your librarian in this library of nightmares, here to guide you through the labyrinth and remind you that the darkest paths might lead to the greatest wisdom. I'm excited about the little nuggets of truth you'll mine from this collection and bring with you on the rest of your journey.

So, whether you are a lifelong devotee of horror or a curious newcomer, I welcome you to lay your bags down at this way station and stay awhile. May these essays deepen your appreciation for the genre and illuminate the power of stories to scare, surprise, and sustain us. Let's love the dark even more—not for its own sake, but for the way it requires us to turn on a light to help us see ourselves and each other.

Sadie Hartmann

Why Ask Why

By Becky Siegel Spratford

"Why" may be the most loaded word in the English language. Why? Because "why" requires an explanation. "Why" is a word of discovery. "Why" is how, as children, we make sense of the world around us. "Why," quite simply, is the key to understanding.

"Why" is also the word to which I have dedicated my entire professional life.

Since the turn of this century I have been a professional book recommender in the field of Readers' Advisory. The crux of this work is matching books with readers through the local public library. And my best tool to not only do this work but also become America's best-known and most trusted practitioner of it is found in that three-letter word, "why." More specifically, figuring out why a reader likes a book and then finding them one with similar traits.

How did I get from the library world to you here in this book, though? For that we need to back up a bit. I began the 2000s finishing up my master's degree in library and information science and cocreating an entire department at the Berwyn (IL) Public Library dedicated to the work of matching readers with their next great read. Beginning in 2004, I returned to my postgraduate alma mater to co-teach the course on Readers' Advisory. As I became the go-to person to train new Readers' Advisory librarians, I eventually left the library proper to become a full-time trainer of library workers all over the world. My focus? Reminding them to center why someone likes a book, not what happens.

I encourage library workers to spontaneously share the books they are enjoying with their patrons. And how does this happen? With "why." I call them conversation starters, but they are really just an excuse to get to "why." For example, I instruct library workers to ask their readers questions like "What is a book you recommend to everyone you know?" and then see what happens. I often encourage the library workers to go first, to show their patrons what they mean by the question, to model the behavior they want to see. So, if this were me working in a library, after asking the question I would say, "For me that book would be *The Only Good Indians* by Stephen Graham Jones, because it is horror, yes, but it is also a heartbreakingly beautiful, lyrical novel about the long history of injustice embedded into our American identity; a tale that begins with revenge and ends with not just survival but hope. What about you? What book do you love to recommend to your friends and family?"

When we ask our readers to share their "why"—more specifically, when we start with questions that demand that "why"—we learn so much more than by just asking questions such as "What is a book you really like?" This direct question is hard to answer for any reader. Also, please notice that my example tells you nothing about the plot of this award-winning novel; it is focused on why I recommend this book. When we encourage conversations that require an explanation, we help readers make sense of what they enjoy reading, which leads us to help them discover more.

And in my case, that "more" leans heavily on horror, because concurrent with the years I spent doing my Readers' Advisory work, I also became the library world's horror expert, most notably through the three textbooks I have written, the most recent of which is *The Readers' Advisory Guide to Horror* (3rd ed., ALA Editions, 2021). These books set out to teach library workers how not to be afraid of horror and its readers. One of my refrains in those books is "Your horror readers are not monsters; they just like to read about them." And how do I do that? You guessed it, I double down on "why." I have chapters on the "appeal" of horror, which is just library lingo for explaining why people like a book. It is based on how the story is told—its pacing, storyline, characterization, frame, tone/mood, language, and style. I walk them through why some readers enjoy being scared by what they read, why they like to feel the fear as it comes off the page and into their bodies. I give them examples of authors and books—dozens and dozens—with annotations that explain why someone would want to read that book. These books are a guide to the genre through the eyes of those who crave it most: its readers.

In 2015, I also began reviewing horror for *Booklist* and *Library Journal*, two of the premier trade journals for book reviews. As a reviewer, I have been given access to horror books before they come out over the last ten-plus years, years coincidentally concurrent with a horror renaissance. I have been among the first people to read—and praise—many books that have become both bestsellers and award winners, from the aforementioned *The Only Good Indians* by Stephen Graham Jones to *Cabin at the End of the World* by Paul Tremblay to *The Devil Takes You Home* by Gabino Iglesias to *The Reformatory* by Tananarive Due, just to name a few. I have been privy to this explosion in great works of horror, stories that are great literature regardless of their genre classification, works that inspire much joy, even as they consciously invoke fear. But I am not just a bystander. I have used my place as a horror expert and critic to get the word out to others, to bring even more readers into the horror fold.

This book is a direct result of that goal. It all began back in 2017. I was in between the second and third editions of my library textbooks and two full years into reviewing horror. I existed in a unique space, with both a thousand-foot view of horror and as someone deep in its trenches. I wanted to use that position to help more library workers connect with more horror readers. I wanted to do something new, something no one had ever done before, something that would be not only immediately useful as a resource but also something that could stand on its own, reflecting the joy, peace, and satisfaction horror readers get from their favorite genre. Of course, I turned to "why" for help as I began a series of invite-only blog posts. I reached out to authors whose work I had encountered in my role as a reviewer and asked them to write a guest post for my library worker training blog, to run during October, the month when the most eyes are on horror. I gave them no further direction than this prompt: "Write me 1,500 words or less on the topic of 'Why I Love Horror.'"

The goal of these posts was for the authors to share their love of horror both as a fan and as a writer. With these posts, I was introducing library workers to new authors and their fiction, but also to their narrative voice. At the same time, I was providing more examples of why certain readers are drawn to horror; those readers just happened to also be its creators. What began as a casual, small project has turned into a much-heralded series with dozens of entries. Authors eagerly await my invitation each summer, and library workers celebrate the access I have given them directly into the minds of authors. It has become an annual horror lovefest, with readers from hard-core genre fans to those who are too scared to pick up a horror book for themselves all taking part. However, while I have loved helping library workers discover why so many readers love horror, I wanted to bring even more people on this journey with me. Once again, "why" was the place where I knew to start.

In this book I have asked eighteen of the top horror authors of this current moment to write an essay letting all of you know why they love horror and explain why they have made it their life's work. The results are as diverse and engaging as the fiction these authors produce. I promise you, whether you are a hard-core horror fan or just someone who is intrigued by its current surge in mainstream popularity or even a big ole scaredy-cat, there is something in this book for you. These authors are some of the top practitioners of unease, discomfort, and terror. They have honed their craft, making up stories that feel so real that the fear jumps off the page and into readers' bodies, leaving them unsettled, tense, and anxious—and loving every second of it. And by asking these authors to articulate why they do this in essays, one after another, together we all come to understand why.

I am eternally grateful to everyone in this anthology. They all took the assignment very seriously, sharing personal stories and deepest, darkest fears. No one paid lip service to the question; rather, they dove deep to the core of their connection to horror as a genre and an emotion. They trusted me with those raw emotions, some of which they have never before shared in public. They trusted me because I am a professional at asking why. They trusted me because I understand horror in a way few others do. And they trusted me because they knew I had proven over many years that I am the perfect tour guide for this terrifying journey.

And now it is your turn. Come along. Take my hand, as I lead you through the minds of today's best horror authors. With monsters both real and imagined, serious trauma, train rides, multiple fractured skulls, a menu that includes light yogurt and chicken nuggets—there is something here for everyone if you dare to follow me.

I will walk you through, whether you choose to read this book cover to cover or skip around to find your favorite authors first. No matter which path you choose, I offer my expertise to light your way. Prior to each essay, I introduce the author and frame their essay for you, including how it fits into the book as whole, and I give you a "start with" title for each author, so those who are new to their work know where to begin, as well as recommending an author for you to try if you already like the author in question, therefore helping those who are fans discover new voices as well. And there are no repeats, meaning eighteen authors quickly become thirty-six.

I have learned so much by asking why—about readers, writers, and myself. It has brought me some of my greatest joy as a Readers' Advisory librarian and as a reader. Let us begin. Let's dare to explore why we all love horror, together.

Brian Keene's Giant-Size Man-Thing

By Brian Keene

Brian Keene is a legend. This book was always going to begin with him, because today's horror renaissance stands on the foundation he has built for all who have come after him. Not only is Keene widely credited with kicking off the twenty-first-century horror boom with his seminal zombie novel The Rising, *but he has taken it upon himself to be the genre's Batman, fighting for good, mentoring young writers, and sharing horror's history, like in the critically acclaimed* End of the Road. *He is also a damn good writer of thoughtful pulp horror featuring fully realized, mostly blue-collar characters, not to mention that his description of the dismemberment of bodies is unparalleled.*

In the essay below, Keene takes readers back to the 1970s and lets them peer into the brain of "little Brian" as he comes to terms with the real horrors in the world, recounts how a certain comic book character got its horror hooks into him, and explains why, for this master of terror, horror remains his best coping mechanism.

Readers new to Brian Keene should start with The Complex. *For those who want to try a similar author, I suggest Christopher Golden.*

———

In the early 1970s, I was a young kid in rural central Pennsylvania. Although I didn't know it at the time, America was going through one hell of an existential crisis. Over the previous decade, our country had nearly torn itself apart over the Vietnam War, Watergate, the Kent State shootings, and the cold-blooded assassination of such figures as Martin Luther King Jr., the Kennedy brothers, and Malcolm X. There were numerous more horrors visited upon us in that time, but to list them all here is to get off into the weeds, and besides, this book isn't about "Why I Love Real-Life Horrors." It's about "Why I Love Horror" as a genre. Suffice to say, as a country, we'd just come perilously close to collapsing, and the divisions revealed in the aftermath of that social, moral, and political upheaval were like great, deep fissures, still belching smoke and hellfire if you stood too close to them.

To this day, I don't think there has been a complete examination of the toll that era had on our collective and individual psyches, but as an adult, and with the benefit of the wisdom that hindsight offers, I can see the impact it had on my parents, the parents of my friends, and the other adults in town. Be it the complete and wanton surrender to drugs, alcohol, or desperately casual sex, or the quiet but no less demoralizing withdrawal into depression, anxiety, or full-blown PTSD, the adults weren't all right. Maybe the kids were all right back in 1966, when the Who released a song proclaiming such, but by 1976, those same kids were grown up and fucked up.

Horror as a genre has always reflected our times. It's a mirror darkly, to be sure, but it always gets things right. When you consider what the genre was reflecting back to us at the time—the early novels of folks like Stephen King and James Herbert; films like *The Texas Chain Saw Massacre*, *The Exorcist*, and *Eaten Alive*—that mirror was obsidian.

My friends and I wandered this American wasteland as half-feral children, roaming unsupervised as far as our bikes could take us, consuming media and substances completely inappropriate for our age, and having a grand old time. Some of my friends had horrible home lives. I knew kids who were abused physically, some who were abused mentally and emotionally, and at least one who was abused sexually. We didn't talk about it back then. We lacked the maturity or verbal skills to do so. But we were aware. We'd all heard Charlie Rich's 1973 hit "Behind Closed Doors," because radio stations were still playing it in 1976, but while the song itself is about sex, we knew there were all sorts of other things that went on behind closed doors. Things we didn't discuss, but things that cast a shadow over everything, regardless.

My home life wasn't nearly as bad as many of the other kids'. Sure, corporal punishment was still very much a thing in our home (I got hit by an assortment of belts, wooden spoons, and—my least favorite— a flyswatter with a wire handle), but my parents weren't abusive. They both did the best they could, and I wasn't exactly a model youth of purity and dignity. Mostly, my parents were struggling with things bigger than my childhood mind could comprehend: my father's time in Vietnam and on riot duty when he returned home, the death of my mother's brother just a few years before, an economic recession and gas crisis, and other stuff. As a result of all that, they could be distant at times. As an adult, I know what my friends were trying to stay away from behind their closed doors. I suspect that, for me, it was that distance I was trying to avoid.

Or perhaps I was trying to fill a void.

And the way I did that was through comic books. I *loved* comic books. Any money I made went right toward buying comics. Any free moment I had, I was reading comic books. On the school bus. While fishing. In all the various clubhouses and forts we built over the years. Under the covers at night with a flashlight, long after I was supposed to be asleep. On long car rides during family trips. On vacation. In church.

My sources were many and varied. Once a week, I rode my bike into town and bought brand-new comics at the local newsstand for thirty-five to fifty cents each. On Sundays, I'd ride my bike to the flea market in another nearby town and buy older comics at a price of five for one dollar. Whenever we'd go on family trips, which were always either to visit kin in West Virginia or to spend a week on the beach at Ocean City, Maryland, I'd hit up 7-Eleven and Stuckey's, often because they used a different distributor from my local newsstand's and thus had comics I normally couldn't find. I read anything I could get my hands on: superhero titles such as *Captain America and the Falcon*, *Batman*, *The Amazing Spider-Man*, *The Incredible Hulk*, *Super-Villain Team-Up*, *Superman*, *Iron Man*, *Marvel Two-in-One*, *Marvel Team-Up*, *The Phantom*, *Justice League*, and *The Defenders*; funny books like *Beetle Bailey*, *Sad Sack*, *Bugs Bunny*, *Mad*, *Cracked*, *Crazy*, and the seemingly never-ending variety of *Archie* titles; educational comics like *Classics Illustrated* and Marvel's knockoff of the same concept; freebies Radio Shack used to hand out about subjects like electronics and rocketry; westerns like *Billy the Kid* and *Jonah Hex*; war comics such as *Sgt. Rock*, *Battle Action*, and *Sgt. Fury and His Howling Commandos*; science fiction and fantasy titles like *Kamandi: The Last Boy on Earth*, *Conan the Barbarian*, *Tarzan*, *Dagar the Invincible*, and *Turok: Son of Stone*; media franchises like *Planet of the Apes*, *The Twilight Zone*, *Star Wars*, *Welcome Back, Kotter*, and *2001: A Space Odyssey*; and horror comics. So. Many. Horror. Comics. Stuff like *Weird War Tales*, *Weird Western Tales*, *House of Secrets*, *House of Mystery*, *The Witching Hour*, *Chamber of Chills*, *Creatures on the Loose*, *Werewolf by Night*, *Monsters Unleashed*, and, of course, the swamp creatures: DC's *Swamp Thing* and Marvel's *The Man-Thing*.

The Man-Thing is the earliest example of why I love horror, in that it was two of his comic appearances that made me fall in love with the genre, resulting in me not only becoming a lifelong fan of horror, but being blessed enough to make my living from it as well.

My introduction to the character occurred when I was in fourth grade. I spent the night at another kid's house, and after his parents had fallen asleep, we stayed up super late, reading (by flashlight) his stack of comic books and a few *Hustler* magazines he'd pilfered from his father's dresser drawer. The only thing I remember about the latter is my surprise that they had cartoons and comics in between the pictures of very naked women, and that seeing those pictures of very naked women simultaneously excited me and filled me with a certainty that I would surely burn in Hell. But while I may have only the vaguest recollections regarding those *Hustler* mags, I can remember every single vivid detail about those two Man-Thing comics I read that night.

The first one off the pile was issue 12 of *Fear*, written by Steve Gerber with art by Jim Starlin and inks by Rich Buckler. I recognized Gerber's name right away. At the time, he was the writer of my favorite comic series, *The Defenders*. Earlier that year, I'd read issue 33 of *The Defenders* and had just been utterly blown away by the entire thing. When I started to read it again, I noticed the creator credit box and saw that it had been written by Steve Gerber and drawn by Sal Buscema, and it had clicked in my mind that these were jobs one could have as an adult. You could make a living not by farming or working in the paper mill like my dad and his friends, but by making up stories. I'd read enough comics in the months since to know that Gerber was my favorite writer. Given my age, I didn't recognize those latter two names. Jim Starlin would go on to become comic book royalty, celebrated for his run on *Captain Marvel*, the creation of Thanos and the eventual miniseries *The Infinity Gauntlet*, and many other career highlights. And Rich Buckler was a name I'd come to later revere almost as much as Gerber's. He cocreated one of my favorite *Defenders* characters, Devil-Slayer, which, decades later, was the first character I ever wrote for Marvel.

But little Brian didn't know any of that. Little Brian didn't know that he, too, would one day write for these same companies, or that, upon the publication of his first novel, he'd exchange correspondence with Steve Gerber himself. He just knew that he liked comics, and he liked Gerber's comics in particular, and this one had a cool-looking monster on the cover.

The story itself tells the plight of Mark Jackson, one of the few Black people living in Topequa, Florida. He's the victim of a racially motivated crime and is being pursued by a corrupt and racist white sheriff. The two characters cross paths with the Man-Thing, who was once Ted Sallis, a scientist attempting to re-create the formula that gave Captain America his powers. Now, Sallis is a moss-encrusted mockery of a man—a monster comprised of mud and slime and roots, a shambling and mindless creature with an empathic nature. The Man-Thing is drawn to emotions, particularly negative emotions like the hatred and animosity that Mark and the sheriff feel toward each other. But there's one emotion that causes the Man-Thing insufferable pain:

Fear.

And whatever knows fear burns at the Man-Thing's touch.

In the time it took me to read that comic, I'd had my first lesson in racism (both institutionalized and blatant) and my first indication that, unlike what my teachers and parents were telling me, not all authority figures were good people. Indeed, some of them were monsters. Because make no mistake about it: that issue of *Fear* may have starred a monster in the character of the Man-Thing, but it was the sheriff who was the real monster.

Then I grabbed the next comic off my friend's stack—the amusingly titled *Giant-Size Man-Thing*, issue 4. (The term "Giant-Size" referred to the page count, which was sixty-eight rather than the normal twenty-four, and Marvel published many of these editions. But *Giant-Size Spider-Man* and *Giant-Size Conan* didn't elicit giggles the way *Giant-Size Man-Thing* did.)

My laughter dried up after reading the first page. In those first few caption boxes, Gerber (aided by a wondrously sinister splash page by Ed Hannigan and Ron Wilson) tells us that, quote: "It is just past noon, but the sky over the Everglades is midnight black and indigo, laced with silvery streaks of lightning. A savage wind rips through the leafy canopy that shrouds the swamp in shadow, and the macabre Man-Thing peers upward through the torn curtain at nature's fury."

Some shit was about to go down.

And boy, did it ever.

Giant-Size Man-Thing, issue 4, tells the story of a kid named Edmond Winshed, a social outcast who'd been bullied or ignored by almost everyone in his life. His parents. His grandmother. His classmates. His high school gym teacher. Indeed, the latter pushed and berated Edmond into running laps to the point that the young man collapsed of a heart attack. At Edmond's funeral, it is revealed that one of his few friends, a girl named Alice Rimes, has possession of his journal, which details the transgressions of his abusers. Alice intends to publish the journal in the school paper. Before she can, the adults conspire to kidnap her. They string her up in the school gym, threatening to torture her if she doesn't reveal the journal's location. You see, these are all good people about town. Edmond's revelations from beyond the grave would destroy their standing. Before Alice can be harmed or probably killed, the Man-Thing shows up, possibly guided by Edmond's restless spirit, and he tears through these monsters. Now, remember, whatever knows fear burns at the Man-Thing's touch, and these adults are very afraid. He burns shut the mouth of Edmond's mother, who never spoke up in her son's defense. He breaks the back of Edmond's father, a man who was always metaphorically on his son's back. And the coach? That heartless, belligerent bully of a coach? The Man-Thing drags him out onto the track and proceeds to burn right through his chest, searing through layers of flesh and muscle and bone, until he ultimately chars the man's heart in two.

That was the moment I fell in love with horror.

The Man-Thing was a monster, surely, but he wasn't the real monster.

Now, as I said earlier, I knew as soon as I read that first comic book—*The Defenders*, issue 33—that writing was what I wanted to do when I grew up. My friends all had their hearts set on being baseball players, or cops, or Evel Knievel, or the Six Million Dollar Man, but I was already training for my grown-up job. I produced dozens of comic books, sitting there at the coffee table in our living room with pencils and a box of crayons, laboring over sheets of defective paper that my father brought home from the mill. I started with pastiches, creating new adventures for Captain America and the Falcon, Kamandi, Spider-Man, and the Defenders, but once I'd been exposed to *Giant-Size Man-Thing*, issue 4? I began leaning toward horror and started inventing characters and monsters of my own, including an intelligent, amorphous space blob I named Bob.

Not long after, on another weekly trip to the newsstand, the latest issue of Marvel's *Bizarre Adventures* caught my eye. According to the cover, it had an adaptation of Stephen King's "The Lawnmower Man." I didn't know who this Stephen King guy was, but Lawnmower Man sounded like a cool comic book villain, so I bought it, took it home, and read it. I didn't entirely understand it (I wouldn't read Arthur Machen's *The Great*

God Pan until many years later), but it struck a chord in me, regardless. I thought it was the coolest thing I'd ever seen when the antagonist gobbles up the dead gopher, but what really intrigued me was the overall sense of menace—of an ancient and inexplicable evil rubbing shoulders with a modern America I knew all too well. It was like *Giant-Size Man-Thing* in that regard. Many of the other horror comics I'd read took place in crumbling old castles or on lonely mountaintops. But these two stories— horror stories—took place in locations I recognized.

When I rode my bike back to the newsstand a week later, I saw a paperback book on my way to the comic book spinner rack. The cover showed a bandaged hand, like something you'd see on a mummy, and it was pockmarked with eyes. The book was Stephen King's *Night Shift*, an important, seminal, historic publication. Like *Giant-Size Man-Thing*, it was full of places and people I recognized. The blue-collar guys slaving away at the factory and fighting mutant rats. The apathetic teenagers partying as the world ended. The cast of "Gray Matter," who could very well have been members of my family. And so many more. Many of the characters in those stories were as bad as the horrors visited upon them. But perhaps even more important to me than the stories themselves was the book's foreword, in which King talked about writing for a living. I read *Night Shift* from cover to cover, and then I read it again. But I read that foreword a third and fourth time. And soon after, instead of just writing my own comic books, I started experimenting with writing stories. On my next trip to the newsstand, I brought home a paperback of *'Salem's Lot*. F. Paul Wilson's *The Keep* followed soon after. Then James Herbert's Rats series. Movies, too, watched late at night on the tiny black-and-white television in my bedroom—*Phantasm, Jaws, Dawn of the Dead, The Omen, Damien: Omen II*, and *The Car*.

Horror had its hooks in me, and there was no turning back.

The genre has brought me a lot of comfort over the years, and it all goes back to that little kid in the 1970s who knew that the world was off, who knew that it wasn't a Disney cartoon, but didn't understand how he knew or what was actually going on. Bad things were happening behind closed doors to kids I knew, and I was powerless to do anything about it? Escape into the safety of make-believe monsters. The nightly news said somebody called Russia wanted to nuke us? Escape into the safety of radioactive mutants. Three Mile Island (just a few short miles away) was melting down? That was okay. I could hide between the covers of something scary, but less scary than that.

Horror, as a marketing category, always does better in times of national or global turmoil. The sales data backs up this claim, as do the trends in horror, stretching all the way back to the gothic and the pulps to now. I would argue that it goes back even before recorded history. If you look at the cave paintings our ancestors made, many of the crude images on those rock walls depict things they were terrified of—beasts that could eat them. Telling stories about those beasts helped them cope and deal. And that has continued throughout human history. Things like EC Comics, Splatterpunk, the '90s boom, the 2000s boom, and today's current indie revolution—all of these were in direct correlation to what was happening in the world at the time. For my generation of writers, we rose to prominence and popularity in the immediate aftermath of the September 11, 2001, terrorist attacks and the subsequent "War on Terror." Why? Because the world was a scary place. People were flying airplanes into buildings and going off to fight wars in places that had nothing to do with that, marching blindly, fueled by the conviction that somebody—anybody—had to pay.

There is comfort in the safety of monsters like vampires, zombies, werewolves, and the like, because those things don't exist in the real world. In the real world, the monsters are shooting up schools and abducting children and raping the environment and rolling back basic human rights and farming our personal lives as data for megacorporations and killing each other based on political opinions or gender or sexual persuasion or the color of their skin. We know these things exist because they happen all around us every day. Real monsters are beating their spouses and children or filming crime victims with their phones for social media clicks rather than calling 911. There is a safety and a comfort in curling up with make-believe monsters so that we can tune out the very real monsters all around us, even if only for a little while.

But horror also gives us a way to talk about and tackle those real monsters. George Romero's *Land of the Dead* is a zombie movie, but it's also about the reign of George W. Bush. Stephen King's *'Salem's Lot* is a novel about vampires, but it's also about the death of small-town America, which was a common fear shared by many at the time of its publication. His 2011 novel, *11/22/63*, is ostensibly about time travel, but at its core is a story about the fear of growing old and of unrequited love. J. F. Gonzalez's *Survivor* is a book about a snuff film ring, but it's really a stark and terrifying examination of what the internet and streaming content are doing to us as human beings and the limits we are willing to push in the quest for more content.

I am in my mid-fifties as I write this. I am far removed from that little boy who was uneasy with the off-kilter world around him, but there are still things I dread. Things I fear. I'm afraid of getting older. I fear for my children and this world they are inheriting from us. I fear that I can no longer protect them and keep them safe. I fear for my parents, who seem to be shrinking before my eyes, growing frailer and more unsteady with each passing day. Over the past few years, many of my close friends have died, and I fear that each passing month seems to leave me a little bit more alone.

I fear.

And so, I still hide inside stories about monsters as a coping mechanism.

And I write stories about monsters so that others have a coping mechanism as well.

I think often about a reader of mine—a young mother in Canada whose baby was diagnosed with cancer while still an infant. For the first several years of that child's life, they lived in a hospital room. The only thing she had to keep her company were my books. I helped, in some small way, to get her through it. My stupid stories about zombies and satyrs and sentient darkness and giant, carnivorous worms helped her cope, helped her find some respite from the very real monster of childhood illness.

On days when the business side of writing for a living is wearing me down, or when the words aren't coming the way I need them to, or when some choad says something unkind about me online, I remember her, and I get back to work.

I'll take the Man-Thing over cancer, or a bloodsucking vampire over a data-stealing corporation, or a demonically possessed girl over a fascist political pundit, or a swarm of killer bees over the spray of a mass shooter's bullets any day of the week.

That's why I love horror.

The Giant Footprint of Horror

By Hailey Piper

Hailey Piper is a rising star in horror. Best known for her tagline "Make Horror Gay AF," Piper's stories, novellas, and novels feature authentic characters whose intentions are always good, even if they make questionable choices. Most of Piper's stories have a cosmic horror element that inflicts existential terror on the reader, an overwhelming sense of unease that is hard to shake, even after the final page is turned. However, the most striking element in Piper's writing is in how she centers love in every work, even as she is actively working to terrify readers to their core, an emotional feat that has garnered Piper legions of fans and much critical acclaim.

Piper's essay, much like Brian Keene's, looks back to her younger self and her obsession with a very famous monster, and how it has followed her throughout her life and brought her joy, a sense of safety, and, most important, the truth.

Readers new to Hailey Piper should start with Queen of Teeth. *For those who want to try a similar author, I suggest Cassandra Khaw.*

———

The obsession began in probably the best way I could've asked for—with Godzilla.

Little Hailey was wild about him. So is adult Hailey, but that's much later. Godzilla was kind of a gateway creature, leaving a trail of skyscraper-crumbs toward that vaster expanse of genre. I found him endlessly fascinating, whether by himself or alongside Mothra, Rodan, Anguirus, and other friends, enemies, and frenemies. Remember the feeling of fascination by itself? We get so caught up in fandoms, sales numbers, and demonstrations of loyalty to brands and intellectual property, it's easy to forget the pleasure of fascination for the sake of itself and for *our*selves, especially from the pre-internet days, when it was possible to have not known anyone else in the world who cared about the things you liked.

One crucial point of intrigue was Godzilla's narrative versatility. I obviously didn't have the words for it as a child, but his movies captivated me in part because, unlike a lot of cinema characters, he showed contradictory facets. I would often wonder why in one movie he was partnering up with a robot that had impossibly programmed itself to change size, while in another he was breaking free from an iceberg to destroy Japan. The pondering never got in the way of my enjoyment—really, it strengthened my interest. I quickly accepted that Godzilla could be a scaly superhero here, a puppet for aliens from Planet X there, and a living horror in his own right, both in the black and white of his original movie or in color in *Godzilla 1985*.

On some level, I would love to think Godzilla's various facets showed me the inconsistency of human behavior, even before I recognized the sometimes violent mood swings of the adults in my life. The latter had no clear explanation to me, whereas years later I noticed Godzilla's older movies had a clear character arc through fantasy stories, science fiction stories, even one spy thriller, bringing him from antagonist to protagonist, then back again when the studio reset the timeline to horror.

I suppose horror was the foundation in both the adults in my life and in Godzilla. That's what I felt, and that's where he came from, and I suppose together, that's where I got a taste for it. Where he inevitably led me.

Soon came *Are You Afraid of the Dark?*, Universal Monsters, and *Goosebumps*, then *Night of the Living Dead*, *Invasion of the Body Snatchers*, Stephen King's *It*, Clive Barker, Shirley Jackson, Stephen Graham Jones, and on and on.

But Godzilla cast his mighty shadow over all. His versatility, complexity, fluidity—whatever you want to call it, because of him, I never took to horror as a simple thing to be frightened of. I certainly was frightened, and often. You don't watch the faux Sam Raimi *Evil Dead*–style monster rampage in *The Unnamable* at kindergarten age (by accident) without a week's worth of nightmares to follow.

Still, the books and movies never frightened me exactly like the world outside the fiction. Rubber decapitated heads and shrieking demons had nothing on bullies, divorces, bombings, shootings, the pervasive anxiety that you're constantly on the verge of fucking up and failing everyone you care about.

Horror brought a joy with its fear even when I was little. That was the key difference. I enjoyed the thrills and felt brave when I could watch anything harsher than a Vincent Price film without hiding beneath a blanket, or make it through Dean Koontz's *Intensity* right after my mother finished reading it.

The joy continues now. There's an excitement in watching an '80s horror movie with an opening credit along the lines of "Creature Effects by," because you know you're going to get to see a creature. I appreciate the sometimes mind-bending imagination and scale of reading cosmic horror, the pervasive clutching of grief horror (and the relief when you emerge from it, like water dripping from your bathing suit when you leave a swimming pool). There's something about coming-of-age horror, in which children and adolescents are often pitted against nightmares that would break an adult's mind, that always feels more accurate to childhood for me than any sweet adventure story. And I love triumphant endings, and bittersweet ones, and dismal doomed ones with the hammer of finality they pound in my chest, after which I turn to the world again. The peculiar melancholy left behind is a kind of comfort. Certainly a catharsis.

In that last, horror knows me. Horror is my grim friend. At its simplest and perhaps most contradictory, I love horror because it's where I feel most like I belong. In its lack of certainty and safety, I'm almost safe.

That probably doesn't make a lot of sense from the outside. You shake horror's toy box and out spill werewolves and demons and masked killers and ghosts and things you can no more easily categorize and rank than our varying human emotions. There's violence, discomfort, loss, and often disturbing questions at the core.

How could anyone feel safe in that discomforting maelstrom? Are you some kind of freaky weirdo freakazoid, Hailey?

Obviously the answer is YES. And that goes right to my point.

I've said a million times or more over the past several years: horror is healing. A concept that's old hat for horror fans, but it's important enough to say again.

In real life, there are horrors without end. You can't stop them by closing a book cover or shutting off a movie. They keep going. But part of horror fiction's beauty, even when it rattles me, is that I can adjust the dosage. I strongly feel there's horror for everyone. I can't say that with every genre I enjoy. Some people just won't accept the breadth of fantasy, or they're bored by romance, and so on.

But even if someone believes horror isn't their cup of tea, there's probably something in horror's purview that they enjoy, even if they give it another name, like supernatural suspense or thriller.

I love that horror can be a refuge. If you've been made at one point or another to feel like an outsider—a monster—then some of the creatures everyone else is so afraid of begin to feel like kin.

It began with Godzilla, but it's carried on from there. I recognized a connection I couldn't put into words as a child seeing King Kong falter atop the Empire State Building. My favorite of the old Universal slate was *Creature from the Black Lagoon* and its sequels. It's hard not to relate as a young queer kid when the Gill-man's home is invaded, himself trotted out for display, and then pushed to match a society he isn't part of in the final film, when they try to make the Creature human. Even the Universal Monsters could be thrown into conversion therapy.

The aim for a lot of fiction is that you'll click with the protagonist. Horror erodes the clean concept of the perfect victim and dissects ideas commonly accepted as correct or normal. John Carpenter's *They Live* is a classic example, in which a pair of shades reveals what's often viewed as ordinary society to be filled with the subliminal messaging of a world dead set on us worshipping money, on consuming, on breeding to keep the machine running. We're told this is normal, but horror asks why is normal *right* when normal looks like cops bulldozing a camp of people just trying to live. What is normal about leaving people to suffer and starve? And then more recently there's *Mister Magic* by Kiersten White, in which an old television show with a sinister core teaches kids how to behave. But it doesn't teach them to be okay with themselves and all their messy feelings, instead insisting on them being always smiley, always polite, as if anger and sadness are abnormal.

And when you feel like an outsider to what's considered normal? You feel a connection with fiction that's willing to poke these bears. It becomes a place of acceptance, not as simple as saying, *This is wrong*, or

Here's the right way to go, or even *That's not normal; here's an example of normal*. It's asking if the concepts of correct and normal can exist on such a simplistic polarity, or if they're really just a pageantry our society cooks up for billboards, industry, and governance.

Yes, sometimes you identify with the human protagonists. Sometimes it's the kaiju, or Frankenstein's creation, or the Cenobites, or the haunted house where the ghosts deeply just want to be left the hell alone.

I love monsters. Ishirō Honda, director of several Godzilla and related films, including the original *Gojira*, famously said, "Monsters are tragic beings." And for a queer woman, for someone who was consistently an outsider as a child and beyond, you feel a genuine kinship with those monsters, those other outsiders. As Honda also said, "People end up having a kind of affection for the monsters. They end up caring about them."

I would hope so. This can range from platonic companionship to other kinds of intimacy. Some characters befriend monsters. A not insubstantial segment of horror fans are known as "monster-fuckers" because—well, it's in the name. When you've been led to think of yourself as monstrous, there's a comfort in fiction that suggests monsters are enjoyed, desired, and loved.

I doubt there's such a person who's never felt hurt or lonely. Horror speaks to this. I feel that is true even in the people who disregard or show moral objection to horror, wrongly believing it will infect and influence its fans to commit horrors ourselves. As if there aren't horrors within us already.

Those unwilling to face their demons may be unprepared when they sneak up from behind. You can pretend they don't exist, but that does not make it so.

Now and then I get questions that together boil down to: Why would anyone want to read or write about bad things happening?

And that's as simple as Godzilla's foot smashing a giant footprint into the street—because bad things have happened to me, and sometimes it's nice to feel less alone. We can show awareness toward the awfulness happening in the world, but reading is a distinctly empathetic experience. You don't even need to dissect adult horror to see this. Look at children's horror. It upsets some people to know it exists. Adults will so carelessly ask, *Why does a kid need to read about a kid experiencing homophobia and racism? Why does a kid need to read about a kid with cancer? Why does a kid need to read about a kid whose parent died?*

Because real kids experience bigotry, real kids get very sick, and real kids lose loved ones. The kids who already need to see themselves can know they're not alone and are understood, and the kids who end up asking questions will learn something about the world and their fellow humans.

Horror doesn't infect us. It *is* us. That's one neat trick of writing fiction, of someone reading or watching horror and becoming discomforted. Now you know how I feel.

And if you already felt it? Then you know you aren't the only one.

I love horror because it is the genre uniquely equipped to explore the vastness of human nature. While horror may show our bodies and lives to be delicate things, meat and bone easily carved up or devoured, our inner worlds are nearly uncategorizable in their intricacy. Horror isn't afraid to explore our complexities and contradictions. I love that there can be books like *Sleep Alone* by J. A. W. McCarthy, its narrative sidestepping the easy right and wrong for its succubus protagonists and instead weighing loneliness versus companionship and how much damage is acceptable when sliding from one to the other. I adore that there can be films like Jordan Peele's *Nope*, which is visceral and captivating but at the same time interrogates how we approach its very medium. It means something that I could write a book like *The Worm and His Kings*, its central conflict focusing on healing and harm, and how these two concepts both dictate and confound our actions, how one person's healing is another person's harm. To heal one, you might have to harm another. You cannot live a perfect life. There is no such thing as perfect, no one correct way to exist. Horror gives us permission to lead readers and viewers down twisting roads and then leave them in answerless places.

These are not simplistic concepts. They take work and self-reflection to better understand, and they don't necessarily have easy answers, if any at all. The more you try to categorize the human experience into neat boxes, the further you stray from its truth.

And horror is the most honest genre.

I love that horror knows, at its center, there is no singular human experience. There are as many as there are and have been people. The same goes for perspectives. One person's nightmare is another's dream. One reader's book that made their skin crawl is the salve to another reader's old scars, a calm they haven't felt in years. One person's simple monster movie is another's haunting depiction of the mass murder one nation has inflicted on another.

When there is so much glinting off the surface of genre's waters, I love horror for delving into the abyss and telling us this darkness knows us and we are welcome in it, whether what rises up from those depths is a reflection of the self, or an irradiated dinosaur, or whether those two concepts are one and the same. That's where it began for me.

A final quote: "Whether for good or bad, Godzilla decided the course of my life."

Me too, Ishirō Honda. And I'm grateful for it.

In the Bermuda Triangle with Sasquatch, Flesh Smoldering

By John Langan

John Langan may not be a household name, but there is a very good chance that he is the author of your favorite horror author's favorite novel of this century— The Fisherman. *A master of works best described as weird, lyrical, and disquieting, most often plying his trade in the short story and novella formats, Langan uses every piece he writes as an opportunity to implant images into his reader's head, ones they cannot shake, drenching their entire body in unease, dread, and fear, but also filling them with awe.*

Langan's essay continues on the theme of the first two in that he looks at the horror monsters and supernatural fears of his youth in an attempt to suss out how they wreaked havoc on his brain and how they have made him the person and author he is today. Langan's piece also showcases his unique narrative voice, as described above, blurring the line between fiction and nonfiction, something we will see more of in later essays.

Readers new to John Langan should start with the aforementioned The Fisherman. *For those who want to try a similar author, I suggest Laird Barron.*

———◆———

Asked why I love horror, my first impulse is to look to my childhood in the 1970s and '80s, to those early traumas and tragedies that happened to me before I possessed the ability to process them. The piece of metal that lodged in the cornea of my right eye when I was two and a half would be a good example, as would the consecutive heart attacks that almost killed and hospitalized my father a decade and change later. To these real-world events, I could add watching an adaptation of *Frankenstein* with my dad when I was far too young (an indeterminate age that was likely around six or seven) and what I think of as the background presence of such films as *The Shining*, *Friday the 13th*, and *The Texas Chain Saw Massacre*, none of which I or any of my grade-school friends were allowed to watch, but whose titles, and the shreds of plot and incident clinging to them, exerted a grim fascination over us. (Someone's parent or older sibling must have seen one of them.) You could supplement this list with movies like *The Exorcist* and *The Omen*, and even more laughable productions like *The Car* and *Devil Dog: The Hound of Hell*, whose diabolical threats assumed an added layer of menace to a kid raised devoutly Catholic, attending Catholic school, in the thick of what we now call the "Satanic panic." (I think *The Amityville Horror* would have been part of this group, too.) Again, it wasn't that I or my friends actually saw any of these movies, but in this case, the priests and deacons who visited our religion class—especially when we were preparing for confirmation—referred to them, sometimes in detail. *The Exorcist* was a favorite, in no small part because it was *based on a real case*, and this assertion, equal parts thrilling and terrifying, rendered the details almost beside the point. What we wanted—*needed*—to know were the signs of demonic possession and the stages of an exorcism, which our clerical visitors provided us in the most serious tones.

Indeed, the more closely I look at my childhood, the more contributing factors I find. There were the TV shows *In Search Of . . .* (hosted by Leonard Nimoy, Mr. Spock himself), *That's Incredible!*, and *Ripley's Believe It or Not!* (hosted with relish by Jack Palance), from whose combined episodes I assembled an ad hoc encyclopedia of the strange and frightening, a kind of secular complement to the infernal perils swirling in the air around me. The Bermuda Triangle; alien visitation, abduction, and experimentation; the Sasquatch and its Himalayan cousin, the yeti; the Loch Ness Monster; Stonehenge; the pyramids of Egypt and the Great Sphinx, with a digression into the process of mummification; spontaneous human combustion; and ghosts: these would constitute a partial table of contents for that personal *Britannica*. Stonehenge was certainly interesting, but its remoteness in space and time from 1970s upstate New York made it more mystery than threat; the same was true for the pyramids, whose construction never seemed that great a mystery to me—at least, not one requiring extraterrestrial intervention. (I was and remain intrigued by the idea of the Great Sphinx predating its adjacent pyramids by a significant amount of time, somewhat like Göbekli Tepe, but that tended away from the unnerving in the direction of the awesome.) As a lifelong fan of dinosaurs real and imagined, I was desperate for the Loch Ness Monster, presumably a plesiosaur, to be real, so much so that when my family visited the loch right before my eleventh birthday, I half convinced myself I had glimpsed the line of Nessie's spine amid a series of long waves rolling into the rocky beach where I was standing looking out at the water. (Every now and again, my mother still asks me, "You saw the Loch Ness Monster, didn't you?" Although each time she does I demur, her continued repetition of the question leads me to suspect she believes in the creature and uses my childhood report to bolster her belief.) (My younger brother and I took home aspirin bottles we filled with water from the loch, as if there were something special about water through which the monster's bulk had swum.) (I don't know what became of those bottles.)

For sheer, creeping unease, though, occasionally climbing to out-and-out fright, the mysteries of Stonehenge and the pyramids, not to mention the delights of the Loch Ness Monster, did not compare with the Bermuda Triangle, the Sasquatch, and spontaneous human combustion. In those days, descriptions of alien encounters/abductions tended to focus less on the probing/experimentation aspect of the experience, so while I found them ominous, it didn't take much for me to imagine a kind of Prime Directive situation in which the reason for these beings' surreptitious behavior arose from humanity's general lack of readiness to meet them, rather than their eagerness to probe our various orifices. (Had I been watching *The X-Files* at this age, I no doubt would have felt differently, but Agents Mulder and Scully's partnership lay another dozen-plus years in the future.)

However, the Bermuda Triangle, a place where airplanes and ships could without warning vanish without a trace, was deeply unsettling. None of the proposed explanations—alien abduction, pirates real or phantom, a portal to another time or dimension—struck me as convincing. All they did was to elide the horror of a place where people simply disappeared into something else, using one mystery to explain away another. There was something about the brute facts of the Triangle that resisted such interpretations. It may have arisen from the dramatizations I watched of sailboats discovered adrift and abandoned. There's also a vague recollection I have of a small boat whose crew narrowly avoided joining the ranks of the missing when they woke in the early morning just in time to steer out of a disorienting fogbank. (Or possibly one or more of them awoke to discover themselves already in the water?)

I think I connected the Bermuda Triangle to that surprisingly widespread threat of my TV and film viewing: quicksand. As represented in shows ranging from *Gilligan's Island* to *Batman*, quicksand was a trap from which the only escape was the timely intervention of a friend with a rope or length of vine. Absent such assistance, you would slowly sink under the substance's surface, unless you struggled and thereby accelerated the process. I didn't know how deep quicksand went, how many bodies an individual pool could hold. I never heard of one reaching capacity. Undoubtedly, my anxiety about quicksand lay in the swamp a quarter mile down the road from my house, whose recesses I, my younger brother, and sometimes our next-door neighbor explored, balancing along the trunks of fallen trees, hopping from mound of mossy soil to mound of mossy soil, trying to keep our sneakers from slipping into dark water, to avoid tearing the big leaves of skunk cabbage whose kingdom this was and releasing their foul odor. I had no trouble picturing myself plunging through a stand of chest-high ferns right into a patch of quicksand. (As you might expect, never was I so relieved as the day I learned you could escape quicksand unaided, largely by remaining calm and slowly swimming to the nearest solid ground.) (Of course, at some point thereafter I learned of the existence of dry sand traps in the desert, but as I have tended to steer clear of the Rubʿ al-Khali, I reassure myself that I am in no imminent danger.) (Still, though.)

What both the Bermuda Triangle and quicksand had in common was the idea that there were places in the world where you could just disappear. Straying into the Triangle seemed to me to threaten a fate worse than death. At least when you died, your soul had a destination in Heaven, Hell, or (chances were) purgatory, while your body remained to be buried in a grave your family and friends would visit. In contrast, the waters southwest of Bermuda threatened erasure, a removal from reality spiritual and physical—existential, an older me might have said. I suppose I could be accused of adding to the story elements not originally present, or at least of focusing on things at best latent in the source material. To this charge, I would have to plead guilty, though I would add that my interpretive extrapolations seem to me entirely in keeping with the kind of responses such narratives evoke from their audiences.

If the Bermuda Triangle was a locus for fears of annihilation so complete it swept you from this life and the next, the Sasquatch was something altogether different, a hulking giant whose roar was an expression of raw fury. My first encounter with the creature was through an episode of *The Six Million Dollar Man*, in which the bionic man, Steve Austin, confronted and fought it somewhere in the mountains. (Of California? Was it the Rockies?) In my memory, the scene alternated between regular and slow motion, the soundtrack a mix of the sound indicating Steve Austin was using his bionic arm and legs (a kind of ratcheting electronic noise) and the Sasquatch's angry bellows. The Sasquatch was shown in shadowy fragments that emphasized its bulk and the threat it posed to the considerably smaller Steve Austin. The episode ended with the Sasquatch tearing off the bionic man's right arm, an act as shocking as it was unexpected. (Anyone who has watched this scene recently, or whose memory is better than mine, will pause me here to offer a correction: it wasn't Steve Austin whose arm was ripped away; rather, he was the one who tore the Sasquatch's arm from him, a significant difference of which I became aware only a few years ago. Up until this moment, I would have sworn I went to bed that night with the vision of the monster wounding the hero replaying in the theater of my mind. Probably, I did. What I think must have happened was I was so afraid of what I was seeing that I looked away from it, several times, with the result that I lost track of the action and swapped what happened for what I was afraid happened. For reasons I can't recall, I never saw the conclusion to the story, which might have helped my misapprehension. As a result, for most of the time that followed, I was certain I had witnessed the hero of the show suffer a grievous hurt, and while the nature of his abilities ensured the limb could be replaced—with maybe a still better one—I felt I had witnessed something awful, something horrifyingly intimate.) For Christmas that year, I was gifted the Sasquatch action figure, and although the toy allowed me to visualize the creature in detail—and at a safe size—its eyes were blank white surfaces, the oddness of which worked against whatever reassurance the figure might otherwise have offered.

Sometime after this, I must have watched the episode of *In Search Of* . . . dedicated to the Sasquatch, where I would have seen the 1967 Patterson-Gimlin footage, ten seconds of film showing a heavy biped covered in dark hair striding along a rocky streambed deep in a forest. I was less than ten years old. In appearance, the creature on-screen resembled its prime-time version, though its bearing was more simian. (I couldn't see its eyes well enough to say with absolute certainty they weren't blank, but it seemed likely.) In attitude, this Sasquatch was the polar opposite of the one on *The Six Million Dollar Man*, walking from left to right casually, casting a disinterested look over its shoulder at the camera, not bothered enough by what it saw to break stride, let alone change direction. The effect of what was presented as documentary footage on me was less dramatic than it might have been, in part, I would guess, because its authenticity was immediately placed in doubt. As is usually the case with films of strange phenomena, most of the discussion around it consisted of reviewing the arguments (pro and con) of its veracity. No matter how compelling the evidence for the footage might be, the necessity of having to establish its truthfulness paradoxically counted against it.

Which is not to say I didn't believe the film, especially when the lights went out at night and I was lying in bed, listening to the sounds outside the windows. The room I shared with my younger brother sat at the northwest corner of the house. Where the north and west walls met, there were three windows, one in the north wall, the other two in the west wall. Alongside the entire north wall of the house, the previous owner or possibly the builder had planted two rows of evergreens, one next to the house, the other seven or eight feet away, beside the neighbor on that side's fence. The tops of these trees reached a little way above the peak of our single-story house's roof, their upper branches overlapping into a canopy that kept the space beneath them in constant shade. My siblings and I called it "the Cave," and at night, it deepened the darkness outside my brother's and my windows. The small sounds of whatever animals moved through it—mice, rabbits, possibly a raccoon—became the footsteps of something dragging its large feet through the carpet of dead pine needles lining the Cave. Yes, our blinds were drawn, but there were gaps at their edges to peer into our room, where the narrow strip of light from the hall light we (I) insisted our parents leave on reached through the door we (I) also insisted they leave open to illuminate the foot of our bunk bed. I lay in the dimness, positive there was something standing on the other side of the windows, a huge presence I could feel as surely as I could my brother sleeping in the bunk below me. I suppose my mind could have given any shape to what I felt watching us, but the Patterson-Gimlin clip offered a form for it with a connection to reality, however attenuated, which gave it an additional terror, while the events of *The Six Million Dollar Man* endowed that form with a savage personality in accord with the threat I perceived (and, yes, projected).

I recognize a correspondence between my embellished Sasquatch and my terror of Frankenstein's monster as he was portrayed in his film incarnations: a gigantic, inarticulate, powerful shape liable to provocation and implacable once angered. (Watching the first *Avengers* film, in which the Hulk chases the Black Widow through the innards of the Helicarrier, I felt a sudden jolt of panic at the appearance of a new iteration of this monster.) The difference was the Sasquatch was real, or something like real, and if I understood that the creature in the seconds of shaky documentary footage was not identical to the one Steve Austin fought, the actual and fictive creatures bled together, until I was convinced if I slipped out of bed, crept across the room, and peeked out the window, discovering an enormous silhouette, its outline fringed with coarse hair—or, worse, a face as wide as the lid of a garbage can pressed to the window, its blank eyes shining with rage, its lips drawn back from its white teeth—it would be about as bad a thing as could happen to me. Despite my nighttime fears, I have no recollection of any concern about Sasquatch stalking the forests and hills around the house. If not from my parents, then I guess I assumed I would have heard news of such activity from my classmates, none of whom could long have concealed such information.

Like the Bermuda Triangle, the Sasquatch was out in the world, and if its existence was unnerving, it was at least not close to me (nocturnal anxieties notwithstanding). Spontaneous human combustion, however, was as near as my own uncertain flesh.

For whatever reason, I recall hearing about this via *That's Incredible!*, an anthology-format show hosted by smiling good-looking celebrities in front of a credulous studio audience. (While my memory groups my learning about the Bermuda Triangle, Sasquatch, and spontaneous human combustion during roughly the same period of time, based on broadcast records, it would appear I did not find out about the third phenomenon until at least four years after the first two.) The nature of this occurrence was there in its name, women and men bursting into flame without warning, the process of such intensity it reduced them almost entirely to ash. It seemed to occur when they were alone, which made sense, as otherwise someone would have tried to extinguish them. Most unsettling, as far as anyone knew, the victim slept or was immobilized through what must have been an agonizing death. There were grisly black-and-white photographs showing the scorched chair in which one person had been consumed (and possibly more?), but there was no good explanation for what preceded these pictures. No one mentioned aliens or cryptids. It was as if the human body had a design flaw, a self-destruct mechanism whose trigger was unknown, but which, when tripped, could not be stopped. Yes, I knew that people died, and I understood the unfortunate event could happen while you were asleep; indeed, how many times had I heard one adult or another opine that this was the way to go, peacefully slipping away? None of these adults had mentioned anything about your body incinerating. (Unless, I realize, the phenomenon started in the brain, which would solve certain logistical problems but is no less horrifying.)

Oddly, perhaps, for a child brought up in the midst of religious belief, the possibility that there might be a divine explanation for the fate that had befallen these people did not occur to me. In no instance did this seem a judgment on a terrible person. Like the Bermuda Triangle and the Sasquatch, spontaneous human combustion appeared an entirely natural, if mysterious, affair. Its apparent naturalness added to its terror. So long as I followed the tenets of my religion, the adults around me taught, I could reasonably expect to maintain God's favor. There was no equivalent catechism for avoiding spontaneous human combustion; it could just happen, like any number of natural disasters. (I realize a more religious reader will fault me for distinguishing between matters of the spirit and those of the [inflammable] flesh, but such was the way my young mind functioned, the divisions it drew.)

As was the case with the Bermuda Triangle and Sasquatch, my interest in spontaneous human combustion did not go away as much as recede, coming to the fore at odd, unexpected moments. During my undergraduate literature studies, I was surprised to encounter the phenomenon in the fiction of Charles Dickens, specifically his novel *Bleak House*, in which an alcoholic, choleric rag dealer named Krook is found reduced to ashes by spontaneous combustion. Within the context of the narrative, the manner of Krook's demise has all sorts of symbolic resonance. Dickens's decision to include it, as another in the multitude of incidents that fill the novel, had as odd an effect on me as if he had attributed the disappearance of a ship to its sailing into the Bermuda Triangle. I wouldn't describe Dickens as a realist, not in the same way I would Gustave Flaubert, but the products of his love for melodrama and sentiment take place in a world approximately the same as the one we inhabit, rendered strange and hyperreal by his style, his talent for elaboration and metaphor. To stumble over spontaneous human combustion as an event equivalent to speaking to a lawyer in his office, or attending a charity function, or practicing with a pistol at a shooting gallery, was disorienting in a way I found difficult to articulate. It was as if an entry from my personal encyclopedia of weirdness had leaped backward in time to the pages of a great work of literature. (You can be sure that when the *MythBusters* hosts turned their skeptical attention to spontaneous human combustion, a quarter of a century after I first read *Bleak House*, I watched the episode with interest, although their conclusion that there was a scenario in which a person could suffer this demise did not offer me the reassurance for which I was hoping.)

In his great novel *The Throat*, Peter Straub writes, "There is another world, and it's *this* world," paraphrasing a statement by the French surrealist Paul Éluard. In what strikes me as a similar vein, Gabriel García Márquez writes in *Love in the Time of Cholera* of a character's "belated suspicion that it is life, more than death, that has no limits." While I don't believe I would or maybe even could have expressed why the Bermuda Triangle, Sasquatch, and spontaneous human combustion exerted so profound a hold on my (fearful) imagination, I think it had something to do with the way in which, separately and together, they indexed a world that was stranger than I saw but not than I suspected, a world that exceeded the limits of my ability to grasp it. No doubt, some of this was due to my age, my developing understanding of and relation to my life. Yet the passage of time—of a significant number of years, if I'm being candid—has not diminished my sense of the world as fundamentally weird, ragged not only at the edges but at patches close to the center, as if reality has its blind spots as surely as any of us. Sometimes figuratively, sometimes literally, people vanish without a trace, are confronted by extreme, unreasoning rage, are consumed whole by internal forces they do not understand. In the face of so outrageous an existence, the probable life proposed by what Salman Rushdie calls "mimetic naturalism" can seem like so much wishful thinking, a fantasy of its own. It's not so much that the markers of the horror field, its favorite tropes and scenarios, are real as it is that the narratives containing them frequently approach the feel of reality, reveal the deep texture of daily life with the sudden flash of metaphor. Probably, it says something about our collective experience of modernity writ large that so many of the narratives of the horror tradition—from Mary Shelley's *Frankenstein* and John Polidori's "The Vampyre" down through their multitude of offspring both literary and dramatic—have continued to find enthusiastic readers and viewers outside the compulsive lists of the classroom. Nor, given the shape of the twenty-first century thus far, do I expect this trend to change.

I don't foresee myself taking a boat through the waters southwest of Bermuda anytime soon; nor do I drink to habitual excess (a proposed contributing factor to spontaneous human combustion). But while I live on the other side of the broad North American continent from where the Sasquatch is supposed to call its home, last night, as I was standing at the front door, preparing to take the dogs out for their final walk of the day, clipping leashes to collars, I heard a series of slow, loud knocks on one or more of the trees outside and across the road. Perhaps you know, this is how Sasquatch are said to communicate with one another across long distances. The sounds were clear, unmistakable. For a long moment, I hesitated, unable to figure out what could be producing this noise in this place at this time of night. The Sasquatch answer had come to me immediately, but even if I gave such creatures any possibility of existing, there was no way one or more of them could be in a modest stretch of woods in the mid-Hudson Valley, was there?

Although the answer was almost certainly not, I opened the door with some trepidation. Gripping the dogs' leashes tight, I stepped out into the darkness, just like every damned fool in every horror movie you've ever seen.

For Fiona

What You Can Learn from Horror:

Don't Run from Darkness; It's Trying to Teach You a Lesson

By Alma Katsu

Alma Katsu is a critically acclaimed author of historical horror and espionage novels. Katsu's horror novels are marked by strong characterization, an excellent sense of place, and diligently researched historical details. Readers will be chilled as the drama, danger, and fear they feel about already unsettling real-life occurrences (like the Donner Party or Japanese internment) is enhanced by the inclusion of the supernatural. Her books are scary but not terrifying and make a great entry point for new readers to the genre.

In this anthology, Katsu's essay marks a turning point, as we step away from the supernatural monsters that helped the first three authors find comfort, safety, and meaning as they came of age, and move on to a subset of authors who grapple with real-world horrors and embrace horror fiction to deal with the fears they induce. Katsu does this quite literally, using her past experience working for various intelligence agencies for the US government, specializing in genocide. As she shares below, this work taught her who the real monsters are. Her writing helps her to come to terms with this knowledge and allows her to better understand how to fight back.

Readers new to Alma Katsu should start with The Hunger. *For those who want to try a similar author, I suggest Silvia Moreno-Garcia.*

At some point in your life, you will experience horror.

Horror may be the only universal emotion. Not everyone will

know true joy or unadulterated happiness in their lifetime (sad as that is to contemplate), but it is a pretty safe bet that each and every one of us knows or will know what it is to be afraid. Whether it comes as a dread chill that freezes the marrow in our bones or a fear that explodes in our brains like an overwrought fireworks display, short-circuiting our nervous system, at some point in our lives we will all know the unpleasant embrace of terror.

Yet there are people who reject horror in all its forms (stories, books, movies, television shows) out of hand. I know this as an author of horror stories. They sidle up to me at the end of talks or when the signing table is being packed up. "I'd read your book, but I don't read horror," they say, usually with a knowing, slightly condescending smile. Sometimes the speaker says this because they feel horror is beneath them. Because they won't expose themselves to it, they imagine it's all like the *Saw* movies or video games. Or they'll protest that we shouldn't dwell on the negative or the dark. This is part of the weird dance our brains do to try to protect us from misfortune. *Don't give yourself over to darkness,* our brains might tell us, like Eric Idle impaled on a crucifix singing "Always Look on the Bright Side of Life" at the end of the film *Monty Python's Life of Brian*.

I'm here to argue against running away from darkness—though I realize that making this argument here, in this book, I'm preaching to the choir. Nevertheless, dear reader, I bet that you are sometimes forced to explain or defend your affection for the horror genre to those who see you as a ghoul or Satanist. Or you don't talk about it at all because you're tired of explaining yourself to people who look down on you from a perch of ignorance.

Too many people regard horror as a juvenile indulgence, right up there with comic books (another shortsighted mistake). They regard it, at best, as mindless fun or, at worst, as indulgence in dark and prurient interests.

I assure you, horror is not silliness. Horror is serious business.

I might have a chip on my shoulder on this point, more so than most people, because I spent my working life in intelligence as an analyst at a few three-lettered government agencies. This was in the 1990s, when the world was boiling over with civil unrest that often resulted in genocides and mass atrocities. Rwanda, Sierra Leone, Somalia, Bosnia and Herzegovina—you name it, I was off in the wings documenting mass slaughter and counting bodies. I won't go into detail, but yes, the job was every bit as difficult and depressing as you imagine. When most people hear the word "genocide," they think of the Holocaust and the Nazi killing machine. The thing you must know is the simple physics of genocide: it's impossible to eliminate a lot of people at one time without the participation of the citizenry. That's right: genocides are mostly neighbor-on-neighbor violence, often with militias providing the muscle.

Consider this your wake-up call. We're afraid of the wrong things. *We* are the monsters.

The average person, particularly the average American, likes to be entertained with fabrications of violence, whether TV or movies or books or video games. Think of the explosive success of TV shows like *The Last of Us* or *The Walking Dead*, video games like *Diablo*, and the devotion of legions of Stephen King fans. Yet, as I've said, you don't need to go to the movies to experience horror: it exists in the world all around us, only it is usually just out of sight. You could catch it in your peripheral vision if you tried, if you wanted to see it. Only most of us don't (though the craze for true crime may be changing this).

Real horror is, well, horrifying. The unreal variety, you see, is only a substitute.

Some argue that writing about bad things is catering to prurient interests, and this is where I voice my strongest objection. Gore for gore's sake exists, of course, but it's not in mainstream horror. I would call it an expression of a *fascination with violence*, and this fascination exists within an awful lot of us, whether we want to admit it or not. But it would be wrong to think that it represents the majority of works of horror, particularly fiction.

To me, horror fiction is not about the horror-inducing act or activity itself but represents an opportunity to explore our feelings about that act. We read a passage that makes our hair stand on end. What is it about this particular passage or scene that causes you—you *specifically*—to be afraid? Why does this speak to you? Usually, it's triggered by something in our past or an unpleasant personal experience. If we run in the opposite direction, away from things that frighten us, we miss this opportunity for self-exploration. We do not grow. We step off the path to self-awareness.

Rather than being a sign of maturity, it's more like an abdication of adulthood. Adults face their fears. Cowards run from them.

Besides, you can't always run from the things that scare you. Maybe it's fun to play this game when you're young. With peekaboo, you know it's really Daddy or Mommy behind those hands. *Boo!* But by the time you're an adult, screaming shrilly every time something frightens you becomes . . . tedious. I have a friend who, in her twenties, would scream like she was being murdered every time she saw a spider. When I asked her how she could be so afraid of a tiny little creature, she shrugged. I predicted that she wouldn't be screaming at spiders once she became a mother, because by then, she would know there were far worse things in life.

You can't—you shouldn't—stick your head in the sand and hold your breath until the terrors go away. Because what if they don't go away? What if they're your neighbors, the very same people you've lived next door to your entire life, now brandishing torches and machetes as they call your name, looking to drag you out of your home and chop you into bits because you're not the same ethnicity as them? And lest you think this scenario unlikely, I can tell you that I cataloged this exact occurrence more times than I care to remember.

That's what a good horror story can give you: a way to deal with your fears. Proof that you can conquer the things that scare you. Helpful ways to deal with your monsters—even if one of your fears is that you'll turn into a monster, too.

That's what's great about the horror we're seeing written right now. It's not about glorifying our innate ability to terrify one another or vying to see who can endure the grossest scene. It's about allaying fears and teaching us to understand where our terrors come from and how to deal with them. This is a little different from the kind of horror story that was written in the past, I think (maybe I'm wrong; I'm no horror scholar), which tended to be long on conjuring up fear and short on resolution. I like that horror writers these days sometimes take one more step with their stories, showing not only that ghosts exist or that there's a vampire in your town, but also showing why the ghost has chosen to haunt *you* or what you can do about that vampire.

Horror is more than a chance to show that a character can heroically stand up to their fears, but that you can, too.

My three horror novels to date (*The Hunger*, *The Deep*, and *The Fervor*) and one of my stories ("The Wehrwolf") have all been historical horror, a subset of the horror genre. It's small but growing, partly because, I think, a lot of readers enjoy seeing a familiar historical event turned on its ear by simply invoking "what if . . . ?" For instance, *The Hunger*, a reimagining of the tragic story of the Donner Party, asks "What if the wagon train had been cursed?" The idea came to me when I started re-searching what had happened on the trail that fateful year, and I saw that *a lot* more bad stuff happened to the wagon party than what typically makes it into history books. They certainly *seemed* cursed.

Early on it became apparent that to simply write a story in which the Donner Party encountered monsters would not be enough. I was asked, "Why would anyone want to read about the Donner Party in 2018, par-ticularly since we know how their story ended?" In other words, *Why is it relevant today?* I've learned in writing historical fiction that there's always a lesson and that we're doomed to relive it if we don't learn from it. (Spoiler alert: we never do.) In the case of the Donner Party, that les-son was to not let class or other petty squabbles divide a group strug-gling for survival. If the Donner Party had supported one another, more of them might've survived the freak winter storm that trapped them in the mountains. (As it was, about half the wagon party starved to death. Some families were nearly completely wiped out, while others suffered no casualties.)

Horror can teach you a thing or two. If you pay attention.

I was even able to revisit genocides and atrocities in writing "The Wehrwolf." Set in the waning days of World War II, it's the story of a young German man whose town is about to be overrun by the victorious Allied forces. He's recruited by the town bully to defend the village by joining a militia, but this militia has a supernatural difference. Once the ungoverned mob gets a taste of violence, though, things spin out of con-trol. It's only after the mob destroys the young man's world that he sees he was a fool to have been a part of it.

Not to get too political, but I wrote that story after witnessing the events of January 6, 2021, after seeing similar events play out in other countries fifteen or so years earlier and thinking that it would never happen in America. If we didn't learn from the Brownshirts (Germany), Interhamwe (Rwanda), or Kamajors (Sierra Leone), maybe we'll pay attention to the Oath Keepers and Proud Boys.

Well, apparently not. Since I wrote those words, the world has moved closer to a bad place, with strident nationalists on the rise and autocrats of every stripe finding new support. It seems to coincide with a decline in curiosity about the world and the censorship of inconvenient histories. Our worst fears are becoming real. Is it because we stick our heads in the sand? Is it because we want to pretend the horrors don't exist rather than face our fears?

That's why I write horror: because of the invaluable lessons it imparts.

Horror Is Life: A Blood-Soaked Love Letter

By Gabino Iglesias

Gabino Iglesias is one of the best authors out there, in any genre, at creating unease simply with how he plays with language on the page. Contrasting scenes of brutal violence with some of the most lyrical and beautiful descriptions to be found in any work of fiction, combined with the use of his native Spanish interspersed throughout his work, sometimes without direct translation, sets an unsettling tone even before readers can start being afraid of the monsters in his plots. Add to this a strong sense of place and complicated, but sympathetic, characters who could readily hop off the page and into your life, and it is easy to see why Iglesias's stories make for some of the most immersive and emotionally charged reading experiences available today.

In his essay, Iglesias expands upon the themes introduced by Alma Katsu, focusing not only on his life in Puerto Rico and his early experiences with horror, but also how it provided a safe space from the racism and hate he faced in the world. And most important, how he used what horror gave him to write himself into his stories, hopefully setting an example for others to do the same in the future.

Readers new to Gabino Iglesias should start with House of Bone and Rain. *For those who want to try a similar author, I suggest S. A. Cosby.*

H orror isn't a genre; horror is life. Think about it. Start at the beginning. Think about your arrival. Before you came into this world, you spent your days floating around in absolute bliss. If all was well with you and your mother, you got what you needed and wanted for nothing. The darkness, which you came to fear years later, held you warmly as you developed. But all good things must come to an end, and what followed for you was brutal. What followed was horror, the very first one. Your introductory anointment, your welcome to life, was not with holy water or oil; your welcoming was done with blood.

Much like the violent explosion that birthed the universe, our arrival into this world is a vicious, gory act no matter what route you take. Option A has you squeezing through a small passage and tearing your mother open. Yes, you will later nap on her chest, get that good oxytocin. But your first gift to her is pain. Option B features a strange creature with a covered face slicing your mother open with a scalpel, yanking you out of your dark, warm paradise. If you don't cry—a perfectly natural reaction to the brutal eviction or slicing excision—the creature who pulled you out makes sure you cry. *Welcome, kid, here's some pain.* And you know what happens after that? Things get worse. Yeah, life is horror.

Listen, before you start thinking that I'm a nihilist, let me tell you this: there is a beautiful cosmic balance out there that makes this horror we call life worth living. For every shanking there are a thousand children laughing. For every broken tooth there is a first kiss. For every sudden, violent death there is a beautiful, auspicious beginning. For every punch you take, if the gods smile down upon you, there are a thousand hugs from your mom. For every injustice there is a ballet of righteous violence. For every tear at least ten smiles. For every monster there is a puppy; for every demon, an angel; for every stroke of bad luck, a bit of help from the orishas. So yeah, life is awesome. Life is the best. But life is also horror, and that's why I love it, live it, write it, read it, watch it, and listen to it.

I hope the sudden appearance of "I" in this narrative didn't startle anyone. This is an essay about loving horror, so at some point there had to be an "I" in here for the whole thing to work, for it to be a personal look into the dark cave of my heart. In any case, I want to talk about my love for horror—yes, the horror that is everything, that exists everywhere— and in order to do that properly, the best thing to do is get biographical.

I came into the world via option B. Seventeen years later I went back to that hospital, found the doctor who had carved into my sacred mother and pulled me by the neck into this world, and popped him in the left eye socket hard enough to feel the crack of his occipital orb. Ah, that ruins the chronological order and is a story for an entirely different essay. Anyway, let's get back on that chronological train. You know, somewhat. Yeah, let me tell you about how I was born into horror and learned to love it early.

One of my first memories is of my grandmother's bathroom. My grandmother lived in a small two-bedroom apartment. The place had two bathrooms, one in the primary bedroom and one in the short hallway. Everyone had to use the bathroom in the primary bedroom. Yes, even the occasional visitor. The bathroom in the hallway wasn't for people; it was for the spirits. The spirits and the saints.

No, my grandmother didn't think the spirits needed a shower, but she was convinced that the spirits lived where you left out offerings for them and that saints stayed wherever you lit big candles for them. Remember that classic cantina scene from *Star Wars: A New Hope*? My grandmother's bathroom was like that, but with ghosts, spirits, and saints.

For my grandmother, spirits and ghosts were real things that we had to acknowledge and, in some cases, defend ourselves from. The spirits of dead family members were good; they came around just to check on you or lend a hand with something. But others could be bad. They could be looking for a body, for someone to hurt. That's why you always have to keep the candles on and have your prayers ready. Walk or drive by a cemetery? Pray so that no spirit enters your body. Hear a spooky sound at night? Pray before an evil ghost attacks you. Horror is everywhere, so learn to live with it. Learn to love it.

My first few nightmares? Also courtesy of my grandmother. She told me stories about what happened to little boys and girls who misbehaved. El hombre del saco. The man with the sack. He'd come and get them in the night. He was fast, too. Little boys and girls didn't even have time to scream for their parents. Nah, the man with the sack would come into your room at night and—*SWOOSH!*—you're in the bag before your sleepy eyes can snap open. Oh, I remember el hombre del saco. I remember all the rules I invented for him. He couldn't get to me if I slept under the covers. I also started leaving things on the floor. That way he'd hit them with his foot and make a sound. If I opened my eyes at the slightest noise, the man with the sack couldn't get me. You know, because the whole thing was that you were in the sack before you could open your eyes. If I saw him coming, I could scream, and my mom or my grandma would come save me. Those nights feeling way too hot under the covers and having the occasional nightmare of a humanoid figure walking into my room and throwing me into his cursed sack were horrible. Sometimes the nightmares weren't that bad, because I would see the humanoid figure slink into my room, but then there'd be a light and another figure, a spirit or a saint, who would come and rescue me from the man with the sack. Ah, those nights were all about horror. They were full of fear. They taught me that the veil is thin and that the whole "that sound was the house settling" thing is just a lie we tell ourselves to protect our fragile psyche. Those nights made me who I am today.

Do you know what happened after those nights full of dread, sitting in bed scrutinizing every shadow and reading way too much into every sound? Well, the sun would come out and I would wake up and my mother's morning hug felt better than anything else in the world and whatever I had for breakfast was great and the birds sang and all was well with the world. Remember that cosmic balance I told you about? I felt it then, even if I lacked the intellect to process it and put it into words. Horror made me appreciate its absence. Horror taught me that after the fear comes the good times, that after the darkness comes the light.

My grandmother's contributions to my early childhood don't stop at spirit bathrooms and men with sacks stealing children in the middle of the night. No, no, there was more. Much more. But I want to talk about school, because with school came an entirely different set of horrors, and my love for horror grew in different ways. First, there was literature.

You see, I was not the best student. My teachers would regularly tell me to leave the classroom and go to the library because I was usually more interested in playing games or having conversations with my classmates than in listening to whatever they were yapping about. In any case, I spent a lot of time in the school's small library.

Every good library story has a librarian, and mine is no different. My school's librarian was named Esperanza. That's "hope" in Spanish. I hope I can one day write fiction as perfect as that. In any case, we called her Epi, and she would always take me in with a smile and let me peruse the shelves and sit down to read whatever I wanted. One day, I found a thin book with a weird cover and a cool title: *Tales of Love, Madness and Death*.

Ladies, gentlemen, and nonbinary friends, Horacio Quiroga has entered the chat.

I read "The Decapitated Chicken," its opening paragraph searing itself into my brain: "All day long the four idiot sons of the couple Mazzini-Ferraz sat on a bench in the patio. Their tongues protruded from between their lips; their eyes were dull; their mouths hung open as they turned their heads."

Through the decades, many other writers would tattoo words on my soul. The opening paragraph of Shirley Jackson's *The Haunting of Hill House*. Charles Bukowski's "Dinosauria, We." A few poems by Oliverio Girondo. Bram Stoker's *Dracula*: "Listen to them, the children of the night. What music they make!" Some Mario Benedetti lines. H. P. Lovecraft's "The Nameless City": "That is not dead which can eternal lie." I could go on and on, but the important thing here is that Quiroga was the first I remember clearly. The words were like punches. Idiot sons. Protruding tongues. Dull eyes. The blood-covered floor at the end. The mother screaming . . . I loved it. I loved every story in that book. I loved horror.

Now imagine this: I was maybe twelve when the brutality of Quiroga's stories changed me in a profound way. I started thinking that it was awesome how writers could make people feel things with words. I started to understand that horror can be scary and make you feel unsettled, but it can also be entertaining. I wanted more, so I went looking with the kind of manic energy some of us put into new obsessions. My efforts paid off quickly. Edgar Allan Poe and H. P. Lovecraft entered my life.

Now I know Lovecraft wasn't a good dude, but I didn't know that back then. What I did know was that getting his books was hard, so whenever a collection of his tales came into my possession, I devoured it like a zealot would a holy text. It brought me joy. I didn't understand all of it because my native language is Spanish and I didn't start learning

English until later in life, but I wanted to know what every word meant, so I got a little dictionary and kept it with me while I read. "Blasphemous." "Accursed." "Ichthyic." "Ululate." "Hitherto." "Batrachian." "Effulgence." "Gibbous." I read, looked up words, and learned. Horror was my teacher, and knowing more made me happy.

Now, just like every essay about how you feel about something must contain an "I" and every cool library story needs a librarian, every love story needs a bit of escalation. Poe and Lovecraft and Quiroga were horrific in different ways, but there was often a supernatural element—or a cosmic one in the case of HPL—that allowed their horror to feel a bit removed from real life. That's when my father, a man with no formal education who has always been a voracious reader, gave me a book he'd gotten from a friend and said, "I'm not liking this, but you're getting into this stuff." That book was Richard Laymon's *Endless Night*. Yeah, there is horror for kids now, but back then you went right from Dr. Seuss to Stephen King's *The Stand*. I was too young to be reading stuff like that and I knew it. That made me love horror even more.

After that initial stage, not much changed. I was hooked on horror for life. Insert here a long montage of my teens. Quiroga, Lovecraft, Poe, and Laymon led to Stephen King, Bentley Little, August Derleth, Bram Stoker, Mary Shelley, Brian Keene, Graham Masterton, Robert Bloch, Algernon Blackwood, Clark Ashton Smith, Richard Matheson, Clive Barker, Peter Straub, and so many other giants. On top of all those haunted pages came the visual stuff. *Jaws*—I was born and raised in Puerto Rico, which is one hundred miles long and thirty-five miles wide with deep blue water all around. *The Shining. The Thing. Poltergeist. The Exorcist. The Serpent and the Rainbow. The Texas Chain Saw Massacre. Misery. Halloween. Friday the 13th. Predator. Alien. Psycho. The Silence of the* Lambs. *Night of the Living Dead. Santa Sangre. The Omen. RoboCop.* (The hand and shotgun scene? Getting blown apart and then turned into a robot so you can get back to work? This is a horror movie and there are no buts about it.) The list, again, goes on and on. I devoured it all. Two things were clear to me: I loved horror, and I wanted to write stories for a living.

Hopefully that's enough biographical stuff to give you an idea of how I discovered horror and fell in love with it. The most important thing is to understand that it never went away. In fact, my love for horror was present in almost every new obsession. Mountaineering and Mount Everest. Underwater cave diving. Cryptozoology. Whatever I got into, it had at least something to do with horror or it was somehow horrific in nature. I loved it all because I wanted to tell stories, and I knew even back then that the more stories I consumed, the better equipped I would be to tell my own. Actually, let's do that right now. Let me tell you some spooky stories that made me love horror even more, yeah? Let's start with the first time I saw a ghost.

Growing up with ghosts, spirits, saints, and the man with the sack and then spending years with my head in a horror book and my eyes on the screen as someone got hacked to pieces or possessed by a demon didn't mean that I saw ghosts every day. In fact, I think one of the coolest things about horror is that we love tropes we know could never be true, so we keep reading and watching as the werewolf transforms or the monster mutates or the demon manages to keep the gate open. I kept reading and watching and wanting to tell stories, which ended up being the only thing I'm good at.

For this story we have to go back to the summer of 2003. I was floating around Florida with a buddy of mine named Willie. We'd worked hard all year at college and saved some money to spend a month bumming around Florida beaches, sleeping in cheap motels, parks, and Greyhound bus stations and on sofas. We were slowly making our way from Miami to Gainesville to visit a friend, doing dumb things and risking life and limb for a good time.

It was early in the trip, so we were still looking for no-name motels instead of sleeping in parks. We had found a twenty-eight-dollar-per-night joint across from Miami Beach, so we splurged. A few blocks from the motel there was a Cuban cafetería where you could get two eggs, bacon, toast, and coffee for $3.50. The second morning we had breakfast there, the man who served us recognized us and said they made a killer Cuban sandwich. Later that day, I went to that place to get a couple of sandwiches before going out for the night.

Outside my room, the motel's hallway had a stained bluish carpet with a horrendous pattern on it, and everything smelled like mold and sadness. I was walking to the elevator, which sat at the end of the hallway, when I looked forward and saw an old man with a full head of white hair, a white shirt, and blue pants walking into the elevator. The old man stepped in and turned sideways the way people do when they're about to press a button on the side panel. The door began to slide closed, so I sped up and called out. The man didn't hold the door for me. However, I managed to put my foot between the elevator's door and the wall. The door stopped and then slid back. As soon as the hole was big enough, I entered the elevator. It was empty.

Seeing that old man and then not seeing that old man was shocking, and shocking things tend to have powerful effects. In my case, it strengthened my love for horror and made me wonder how many other things could be real.

Don't worry, I won't regale you with another ghost story, though I do have more. No, instead, I will tell you that loving horror, for me, meant studying horror, consuming horror, and wanting to create horror. Loving horror meant thinking about it, about its ubiquitous nature, about the way it seems to be woven into the very fabric of the universe.

More years went by. I moved to the States. I wrote horror. I published some short stories. Then I published some novels. I hustled for fourteen years, because horror was no longer something I loved; it was what I wanted to do with the rest of my life. Finally, a decade and a half later, I became a full-time writer. I won a Bram Stoker Award and a Shirley Jackson Award. I became the horror columnist for *The New York Times Book Review*. I am regularly asked to teach horror at universities and conferences. I was born into horror, and horror is my life.

There are many things that could be said here—about horror, about my journey, about life—but brevity, according to a different William, is the soul of wit, so I'll do something else, something shorter and more dynamic. Yes, I will give you a list. Lists are great because they force you to be succinct, to be clear and get your point across in a few words. Here, in no particular order, are ten reasons I love horror:

- I love horror because most of the horror I read when I was younger was about fear of the Other and now it's about a lot of things, including about the experiences of the Other.
- I love horror because there were no people like me in the stories I read, but writing horror stories gave me the power to write myself into existence.
- I love horror because it is a perfect mirror we can hold up to society. It is a tool we can use to criticize, to educate, to suggest solutions.

- I love horror because of the work of the brilliant folks who make contemporary horror the best genre around. Their names would fill hundreds of pages, but believe me when I tell you this: we are living in the new golden era of horror.

- I love horror because it now pays for my house and my food. It has given me many friends, many cool events, and many amazing conversations about what horror is, what it can do, how we can use it to change the world.

- I love horror because it is at the core of everything that exists. Don't believe me? Let me break it down for you. Let's start with something very small: a single Marburg virus particle, which is only about eighty nanometers in diameter. You know what that microscopic thing holds? A future death covered in blood. It holds pain, convulsions, internal bleeding, as well as bleeding from all mucous membranes. That is horror. Now think of the biggest thing we know, the Hercules–Corona Borealis Great Wall, a massive cluster of billions of galaxies that would take you ten billion light-years to cross. You know what lives in those galaxies? No, you don't. But I assure you whatever lives there comes from the same violent beginning, so whatever is there is also horrific. All that darkness, all that emptiness, all that cold, all those creatures, those timeless entities floating among the bright ghosts of dead stars. Always remember what the great Werner Herzog said: "The universe is monstrously indifferent to the presence of man." We are but a speck of dust floating in an expanding, infinite universe. If that's not horror, I don't know what is.

- I love horror fiction because it's controlled chaos. It can teach us survival skills—don't solve the puzzle, don't touch the mysterious goo, don't read that book out loud if you don't know what you're saying—while helping us develop empathy.

- I love horror because horror is more than a word, more than a genre: horror is a community, a lens, an aesthetic, a shape-shifting vibe, a tone, an atmosphere, a feeling, a way of life.

- I love horror because horror never judged me, never called me a slur. Horror was there in Spanish and then in English. Horror took me to France, where I stood on a sidewalk in the middle of the day with tears running down my face because my words took me to France to share my horror stories with a new world of readers.

- I love horror because when the folks in the ivory towers said it was a lesser genre, horror didn't care. Instead, we built something better, something unique and endlessly entertaining, gripping, important. When they said horror couldn't eat at literature's table, we horror folks built a table from the bones of our enemies and welcomed everyone who wanted to join us.

I could go on, but I won't. Instead, I will let you sit with the idea that horror is part of everything. Horror was there at the beginning and it still is. It's also there at every end. Horror is a movement, a home, a place to be reclaimed. Horror is our beloved collection of tropes—demonic possession, werewolves, ghosts, vengeful spirits, vampires, zombies, haunted houses, final girls, masked killers, hungry monsters—but also a space to process trauma and learn from each other. Horror is in your veins, riding in the memories your DNA carries from a time when we sat around the fire and made up stories about the hungry eyes that looked at us from the edge of the darkness. Those eyes are still out there, and we are still telling stories about them because telling stories is how we understand the world.

From the possible chaos at the tiny hearts of quarks to the black nightmares waiting on the other side of black holes, horror is everywhere. It's always been there and it will always be there, so we embrace it and learn to love it. So the next time you turn the light off and run to your room before that thing that lives in the kitchen gets you, or the next time you tell yourself that the steps you heard are just the house settling, remember that you're not alone, that we are all right there with you.

Next time someone talks to you about horror, remember that it was there from the beginning and it will be there when the sun scorches the earth. Horror is what we came from and what we endure. Horror is home.

My Long Road to Horror

By Tananarive Due

Tananarive Due has been writing suspenseful, fast-paced horror that has an unapologetic social justice lens since the waning days of the last century. Her chilling and terrifying works of supernatural evil in many forms (zombies, witches, ghosts, and immortal evil creatures—she has dabbled in just about every subgenre) are grounded in the Black experience, including themes of racial discrimination, family dysfunction, and ancestral traditions. In her work as a professor, Due has written and lectured about the uniqueness of Black horror in many spaces, from the classroom to major newspapers to documentary films. Her expertise on this topic alongside her evocative and chilling stories have made her one of the genre's current stalwarts.

In this essay, Due continues the theme of the last two entries, as she contemplates her experiences as a Black woman and a child of parents who fought in the civil rights movement, and how she came to understand that all her work is not only inextricably linked to the Black experience but also how it is responsible for her success—a realization she came to with the help of Jordan Peele, yes, but also an important conversation with Anne Rice.

Readers new to Tananarive Due should start with The Reformatory. *For those who want to try a similar author, I suggest N. K. Jemisin.*

———

In my first horror graphic novel, *The Keeper* (with Steven Barnes, illustrated by Marco Finnegan), I came as close as I ever have to capturing the moment that drove me toward horror when I was only about eight years old. The night I stared Death in the face.

My family was visiting my great-grandmother Lydia in Indiana, and because of lack of space I shared a bedroom with her. I loved my great-grandmother—a cheerful storyteller who was eager to pass on family lore to me—but in the shadow of night, all I heard from her bed beside mine was the rhythmic *hisssss* of her oxygen machine. (She had emphysema, so she used a machine at night to help her breathe.)

All night, I was terrified. What if she stopped breathing overnight? What would I do?

Then, an even more insidious and horrifying thought: *Will I have to sleep with an oxygen machine one day too?* That night with Grandmother Lydia, as we called her, was my first exposure to serious illness. And as we lay in twin beds and I stared up at the inky ceiling in a strange house listening to that steady, ominous hissing, the certainty rocked me like a thunderclap: *I'm going to get old and die one day too.* The thought sent me spiraling helplessly into a loop; once it was in my mind, I could not expel it. I have not expelled it since.

Meeting mortality up close in my great-grandmother's bedroom— really understanding, perhaps from photos around the house, that she had once been a little girl just like me and that one day I would be an old woman just like her—changed my life forever.

That was my first moment of pure horror.

But I might not have made the leap between true-life horror and horror movies and literature without the influence of my late mother, Patricia Stephens Due, who was the first horror fan in my life. My mother's first moments of pure horror probably were related to her upbringing in Jim Crow Florida—whispers of stories about disappearances or lynchings, or the dehumanizing presence of "Whites Only" and "Colored" signs that offended her spirit from the time she was a child defiantly ordering ice cream from the whites-only window with her sister in Belle Glade, Florida.

They later went to college at Florida A&M University together, and they made history as civil rights activists. My mother and her sister, my aunt Priscilla Stephens Kruize, were among eight Florida A&M students who spent forty-nine days in jail rather than pay their fine after a sit-in at a Woolworth's lunch counter. My mother was also among the activists who lay down in front of garbage trucks to support striking sanitation workers in 1968—the cause for which Dr. Martin Luther King Jr. ultimately gave his life. Likewise, my father, working as a legal observer in Mississippi during Freedom Summer in 1964, had been pulled over and detained by the very sheriff who likely had tipped off the Ku Klux Klan about where to find the Black activist James Chaney and white allies Andrew Goodman and Michael Schwerner—who were murdered for trying to register Black people to vote. (Both of my parents had met Schwerner before he died.)

We heard some powerful stories growing up. Despite my Gen-X rose-colored glasses, we lived through some powerful times with them. Death threats from neighbors. A call from the FBI warning my father that he might be the target of a racist serial bomber. As I look back on it, no wonder I learned to love horror. Although my parents never told us about the death threats when we first integrated our Miami-Dade neighborhood, inspiring white members of their Unitarian church to sit watch over the house at night, we felt the isolation. The stares. Much horror is rooted in isolation.

And my mother's favorite tonic for her racial traumas was horror movies. While I was working as an executive producer on the Shudder documentary *Horror Noire: A History of Black Horror*, I realized that my mother was not alone. In many Black families—and no doubt in many families period—horror served as a balm to soothe the trauma of being outsiders in our own nation. So although much horror cinema either excluded Black characters or turned them into stereotypical tropes like the first to die, the spiritual guide, or the magical Negro, Black horror fans found it soothing to see monsters, demons, and ghosts on the screen. Fictional scares could serve as both emotional validation for the way prejudice and poverty made people feel, and a way to vanquish fictitious monsters in a way white supremacy could not be vanquished.

At the very least, horror movies gave viewers examples of characters who learned how to run away from or stand up to overwhelming terror. I imagine that those examples gave my mother the strength to carry on the real-life battles against human monsters like the Tallahassee police officer who deliberately threw a tear gas canister in her face when she was only twenty years old—an event she never entirely healed from. For the rest of her life, my mother suffered a sensitivity to light that forced her to wear dark glasses even indoors most of the time.

So, of course my mother introduced me to Saturday afternoon Creature Features, old black-and-white films like *The Mummy*, *The Wolf Man*, and *The Fly*. She was drawn to the images of tragic monsters hunted by society because they were scary, because they did not fit in. (And, yes, maybe the Wolf Man did kill a few people during the full moon, but wasn't he also just misunderstood?)

My first memory of a real scare in a horror movie (also no doubt at my mother's side) was in the 1958 version of *The Fly*, with Vincent Price, about a scientist who is part human and part fly, at war with his own nature. The iconic ending is seared into my memory: a creature with a fly-sized body and a human head trapped in a spiderweb while a spider stalks him, calling, "Help me! Help me!" in a voice too tiny to register to the person sitting so nearby.

The portrait of invisibility. Being unheard. Being dismissed. I was chilled to my toes.

When I was sixteen, my mother gave me my first Stephen King novel: *The Shining*. The paperback with the silver cover.

Finally, I was home.

But my journey from being a horror fan to actually writing scary stories myself was a long one—and, in a way, presented a very different kind of horror story of invisibility.

A story of losing my voice. Of losing my way.

The power of Jordan Peele's *Get Out* in 2017 reminded the world of the power of horror to tell stories of social impact, holding up a fun-house mirror to our world so we could better see ourselves through the distortions. Even in earlier horror cinema, depictions of subjugation in a film like *The Mole People* (1956) reminded me symbolically of American slavery, with an allure on that basis alone. Dr. Robin R. Means Coleman, author of *Horror Noire: A History of Black American Horror from the 1890s to Present*, also points out powerful metaphors of race in *King Kong* and George A. Romero's *Night of the Living Dead*.

In hindsight, it would seem that I would have been attracted to horror writing all along, recognizing the nexus between my family's civil rights history and the power of fantasy to help express its emotional impact.

Far from it.

My most recent novel, *The Reformatory* (2023), has been the most successful book launch of my career, which began with the publication of *The Between* in 1995. Set during Jim Crow in 1950—and loosely inspired by the true-life history of my great-uncle Robert Stephens, who died at the notorious Dozier School for Boys in Marianna, Florida, in the 1930s—it's the story of a twelve-year-old Black boy, Robert Stephens, who is unjustly sent to a haunted reformatory. In the course of the novel, partially through the story of his older sister Gloria's efforts to free him, Robert and the reader will learn that the "haints" are far less scary than the story's human monsters and the bigger monsters of bureaucracy, complicity, and white supremacy that allow the reformatory to continue to kill and traumatize children.

If I could go back in time and reveal to the aspiring writer I was in my late teens and early twenties that I would one day win major literary prizes for writing a horror novel set in the rural Jim Crow South, I wouldn't have believed it. And I'm certain that every history teacher I ever had would be surprised at how much I have embraced history in my writing.

It has been a long, circuitous journey.

My Black literary idols were Toni Morrison and Alice Walker—but although I admired their storytelling, as an aspiring author their stories did not seem to be my stories. I grew up in suburban Miami. In air-conditioning. I didn't know anything about rural life except for the ducks that swam in the backyard canal where my country-bred mother fished with a cane pole, a whisper of her childhood she shared with me—mostly because I had a knack for getting the worms on the hook (that memory made its way into *The Reformatory*).

As a part of Generation X, my struggles against racism were not the flagrant "Whites Only" and "Colored" signs and exclusion of every

African American generation before mine, but the more ambiguous eyes of store clerks following me as I shopped; neighborhood kids calling us the N-word—some as young as five, others years older than I was—when we integrated a neighborhood in the 1970s; my first Black Lives Matter moment when the police officers who murdered the unarmed motor-cyclist Arthur McDuffie were acquitted when I was fourteen; and, yes, that time I was in college driving through Georgia with my mother when the highway patrol officer ultimately did jump-start our stalled car—but when I first went up to his window to explain why we had pulled over to the shoulder, he did not look my way or speak a word to me, as if I were invisible (and that was the moment when I realized why my parents had forbidden me to drive from Miami to Lexington, Kentucky, alone).

So, yes, there was racism, but I was also sheltered from it, especially when I compared it to my parents' stories of 1960s civil rights activism, of bullets, fire hoses, and tear gas. Or my father's memory of his entire second-grade class bursting into tears when their teacher walked them to the movie theater to see *Snow White and the Seven Dwarfs* only to be turned away because they were Black. (The memory still brings a tear to his eye, and he is now in his eighties.) My experiences certainly did not feel like the fodder for novels like *Sula*, *The Bluest Eye*, or *The Color Purple*.

What I really wanted to write—although I hid it from myself for years in creative writing classes—was supernatural horror. As a child, Alex Haley's *Roots* had electrified me with its possibilities in shining a light on forgotten history, but I never imagined myself as a historical writer after about the age of ten, when I wrote handwritten passages in a *Roots*-inspired Middle Passage story I called "Lawdy, Lawdy, Make Us Free." After that, my childhood writing was about heroic and often fan-tastical adventures. I naturally should have drifted to horror.

But I learned about genre bias early in my creative writing life. As a student in an undergraduate workshop at Northwestern University, where I had wonderful instructors, we were asked to name two of our favorite authors: I named Toni Morrison and Stephen King—one the warrior queen fighting to give voice to Black experiences with her sword of razor-sharp language and perception, the other the King of the more mundane frights that felt, on some level, like literary validation of any fear or trauma we have buried in ourselves.

But you should have seen the looks on my classmates' faces when I mentioned Stephen King's name at that workshop. That was how I learned about genre bias—and I never mentioned his name again. I wanted to learn what a "real writer" was supposed to write. Like I always had from the time we integrated that neighborhood, I wanted to fit in.

But I was an author without a literary home. I was sure I would feel like a fraud if I tried to write like my idols Toni Morrison and Alice Walker ("suburban" Black fiction was not a category on any bookshelf anywhere). How did one become a "Black author," with that voice of wisdom and authority and kitchen tables and history conjured to life?

And it had not dawned on me consciously that I wanted to write horror. Why should it? If Stephen King himself couldn't cut it in the eyes of my peers, why should I bother? We were reading Raymond Carver and Joyce Carol Oates, and in addition to their craft lessons, which are numerous, I began to develop the notion that a "story" was about a white person coming to an epiphany. Me! Raised by civil rights activists! Our home library was brimming with Black history books—even Black history comic books!

After exposure to "canon," I erased myself from my own imagination, in terms of both race and genre. Not intentionally. Not for the sake of sales—I was still trying to craft scenes and build characters, so my mind was far from thoughts of marketing and promotion. Where my childhood writing had been deeply personal, by college and grad school I was falling away from myself in my writing. My protagonists became white women and mostly white men. My writing was a mimicry of a sensibility cleansed of the inheritance of US slavery and Jim Crow: I wrote Jewish characters and queer characters, drawn to their kindred marginalization, practicing writing with empathy—but after grad school, halfway through a novel called *Separate and Related*—a title I still quite like—I ran out of imaginative fuel. The novel was about a gay white male New York playwright who is diagnosed with leukemia and must move in with his estranged older brother, thus reestablishing their relationship.

I was nowhere to be found in this novel. Beyond a summer internship, I had barely visited New York, much less lived there. I wasn't a playwright. I wasn't gay. I'd never had any chronic disease. I didn't even have a brother. Although it was one of my first experiences of seeing characters come to life on their own during a scene with dynamic conflict, a *ping* that I was becoming a professional-level writer, I had nothing left to feed that novel. I could have done the research if the burning core had been expressing something about me and my own experiences—but it had nothing to feed me either. No answer to the question: *Why* are you telling this story? Why are *you* telling this story?

Writers need a "why" to fuel the work we do. I'd been so busy with craft lessons that I had lost track of the reason I wanted to write. I had lost my voice before I had the full opportunity to explore it.

Then two things happened: I read *Mama Day* by Gloria Naylor, which was the first time I had read a novel of the metaphysical with contemporary Black characters. (Somehow, at that time, I had not yet come across the great Octavia Butler.) Naylor's work gave me a model in such an electrifying way—city characters who felt cut off from their country roots—waking me from my racial slumber. Magic and healing. But *Mama Day* wasn't the full-out horror I felt myself wanting to write. No one called it "horror." And my lingering fear was that if I began to publish horror stories, I would bring some kind of shame to my family legacy.

You have to understand: my parents were John Dorsey Due Jr. and Patricia Gloria Stephens Due. Their names were in the indexes of my college history textbooks. And I'll say again: my mother was a horror fan. And she had made it clear to me that she would not be disappointed if I pursued the path of an artist rather than, say, going to law school like both of my sisters, Johnita and Lydia. She gave me a *Writer's Market* for my birthday every year. She made it a point to tell me that during the days of police dogs, fire hoses, and church bombings in the 1960s, the NAACP put effort into building its Beverly Hills–Hollywood branch because it believed in the power of representation. I had permission from the people I cared about most to pursue whatever my writing dream might be—as long as I got that journalism degree so I could get a job, back when that was a stable career path.

But even so, I hesitated. I wrote the surreal, but not quite horror. Not yet.

Then I was assigned an interview with the author Anne Rice for the newspaper where I worked for ten years, the *Miami Herald*. I read *The Vampire Lestat* to prepare for our phone interview, and I came across a profile with the same genre bias I had encountered in college—the author was arguing that Rice was "wasting her talents writing about vampires."

So, without telling Rice that I was an unpublished writer, I asked her how she responded to that criticism—and held my breath, waiting for her answer.

I've told this story many times over the years, and most times I've told it wrong, because I reduced it to her telling me that her books are taught in colleges and that writing the supernatural gives you the freedom to explore large themes like death and loss. That's all true—but that wasn't why I was so inspired that I finished my first horror novel, *The Between*, nine months later. Here is what Anne Rice said to me:

"Everybody knows who Jane Eyre is. Mary Shelley, everybody knows who she is, and everybody knows who Frankenstein's monster is. These are great, powerful, heroic images that really allow you to go outside yourself, to really talk about questions that change you.

"That's what Homer did for the people who went down to the corner tavern to listen to him. They didn't know Achilles, they didn't ever see the walls of Troy, but they sat there and listened to him talk about these enormous heroes and these enormous conflicts. And it was not just escape, but it was an escape that improves you. You go back feeling different, and that's what literature should do."

Ultimately, I agree with Anne Rice. I agree with Jordan Peele.

Horror makes us come back feeling different—oddly enough, feeling *better*.

Feeling seen. Feeling validated.

Feeling.

That is why I love horror.

Monster Girl: How Horror Gave Me a Place to Belong

By Jennifer McMahon

Jennifer McMahon expertly straddles the line between thriller and horror. Her compelling, twisty, and suspenseful novels feature engaging characters, strong female leads, and plotlines that often jump back and forth in time, which serves to ratchet up the tension and fear. The supernatural plays a role in all her work, with some titles featuring it more heavily than others. McMahon is read by many people who do not consider themselves horror fans, as her numerous appearances on the New York Times *bestseller list attests to, but it is impossible not to see the provocation of fear that is at the heart of all her stories.*

McMahon's is the final essay in this set of pieces where the author looks at the horrors in their immediate world and uses the genre to help find peace and acceptance. For McMahon it was the power horror gave her while living with a mentally ill mother, facing constant bullying, and coming to understand how different she was from the other girls around her. When she first watched and then started writing horror, McMahon saw it gave her a power over the fear, it gave her a place to belong, and, quite simply, it made her brave.

Readers new to Jennifer McMahon should start with The Winter People. *For those who want to try a similar author, I suggest Simone St. James.*

When I was in third grade, I did a spell to become a werewolf.

I grew up in my grandmother's house in a little suburban town in Connecticut where all the kids at school seemed to have a mom, dad, station wagon, and membership at the country club (which had a way better pool than the public park where my grandmother took me for swimming lessons). The dads worked for the insurance companies in Hartford. The moms stayed at home making balanced lunches they packed neatly into cute lunch boxes, baking after-school cookies from scratch, and taking their daughters to the salon for perfect Dorothy Hamill haircuts. I saw my dad only on Sundays and holidays. My mom was in and out of hospitals and drunk tanks. I wore boys' Sears Toughskins and had wild hair that I refused to let my grandmother comb. Our backyard was bordered by woods, and I spent most of my free time exploring, searching for monsters that I was sure were out there, hiding just out of sight.

By third grade, I was starting to realize that there was something *else* different about me. When I played House—or better yet Hospital (which I loved because terrible things always happened)—with a group of girls, I always begged to be the boy character. That way I got to marry a girl, maybe even kiss her on the cheek or hold her hand—preferably as one of us lay dying on an imaginary hospital bed.

I was a fearful and anxious kid, but I loved ghost stories and monster movies. I was obsessed with all the classic Universal Monsters movies: *Dracula, Frankenstein, Bride of Frankenstein, The Mummy, The Wolf Man, Creature from the Black Lagoon*—particularly those with monsters who are humanoid in form and are bound to the world of the humans. They may have even been human once, but they've sprouted fangs or fur or fins and have transformed into something horrifying. They're creatures who don't belong; creatures who dwell at the fringe; creatures who are feared—often hunted and killed—because of their strangeness, their *otherness*.

I felt more than a little monstrous myself back then, carrying all my secret inner thoughts and worries, unsure of where or how I fit into the world, and I often daydreamed of actually *becoming* a monster. I wished for it. I willed it. I wanted to shed my human skin and all my messy human emotions and go full-on monster. I put on monster masks and jumped out at friends and family. I had a book on monster makeup and spent hours practicing: painting my face various shades of green, sticking oatmeal and honey to my skin, drawing scales on my cheeks with my mother's best eyeliner, making bulbous eyes from egg cartons and taping them over my own. But all this was dress-up. Rehearsal.

I knew, just knew in my bones, that real monsters existed, that they were out there. And if I was going to find true evidence of them anywhere, it would be in the library. I loved the library. I felt at home there, surrounded by books and quiet, getting to pick up and read whatever I wanted without being questioned by a teacher or some other well-meaning grown-up. The Avon Free Public Library was a little stone building in the center of town. I could bike there, check out books, then head over to the Tinkers Drum Country Store in Old Avon Village and load up on penny candy. Back home, I'd hide out in my room, in a corner of the basement, or up in my tree fort and pore over the library books while devouring Bit-O-Honeys, Mary Janes, Red Hot Dollars. When I found the book on werewolves on the library's shelves, complete with a spell in the back for how to transform yourself into a werewolf, my skin tingled. I knew it was fate. This was not a book full of made-up stories. This was real. Real stories. The true history of werewolves and shapeshifters. And in the back, a real spell that came with a stern warning not to enter into this endeavor lightly.

I was ecstatic.

That afternoon, as I sat locked in my room studying the spell, I knew everything was going to change. I was going to say goodbye to my stupid human life and become the monster I'd always felt lurking deep down inside me.

On the next full moon, I crept out of bed, snuck out my window, and went to a clearing in a circle of trees deep in the woods behind our house. I lit a candle, recited the words, and waited. And waited. Nothing happened. I did not sprout so much as a tuft of fur or a single fang. When I gazed up at the moon, I wasn't overcome with bloodlust, my human-self a distant memory as my animal-self took over. I crept back to my room and into bed, profoundly disappointed to still be a mere human girl who had to wake up in the morning, eat her Cheerios, and go to school and do her best to pass as a normal human.

It wasn't long after my failed attempt at transformation that I found a copy of *The Amityville Horror* on my mother's bookshelf and snuck it into my room to read under the covers by flashlight—the way I read all books that I knew I wasn't supposed to be reading, like my grandmother's medical textbooks. I was fascinated by the photos and descriptions of terrible diseases—syphilis, smallpox, leprosy—but the story *The Amityville Horror* told was so much more frightening than all those illnesses. I was both mesmerized and terrified. Jodie the pig, the red room, the flies! And the most terrifying part of all was the subtitle, in thick red letters on the dust jacket: *A TRUE STORY*. I read it and reread it, memorized my favorite parts. I tormented my younger brother by telling him *Amityville Horror* stories at bedtime.

I brought the book to a birthday slumber party. I didn't know the birthday girl very well, and it was clear that her mother had made her invite me. I didn't have many friends, and the invitation seemed destined to move me up in the ranks of the social strata of Towpath Elementary. We ate our pizza, played our party games, sang "Happy Birthday," and ate a Carvel ice cream cake. Then we went up to our hostess's bedroom, unfurled our sleeping bags, and settled in for Truth or Dare and swapping secrets. That's when I brought out my new favorite book, and I told them I had something really scary to share if they wanted to hear. And they did. So I told them all about the house in Amityville, I told them what happened within those walls, swearing it was a true story, that evil like that really did exist. I read them choice passages about the flies and Jodie the pig. By the end of my reading, two of the girls were crying. Someone had turned the lights back on, and the birthday girl raced downstairs with her crying friends to find her mother. I was not invited back; nor was I chosen for many sleepovers after that.

But something else happened, something bigger. I realized the power that fear could have and the thrill that came with being the person in control of it. The person who dared read the scariest passages aloud. The person who showed those poor girls just what might be hiding on the other side of the veil.

It was around this time that I wrote my first short story, "The Haunted Meatball," for a school assignment. It was about a boy who is pursued by the glowing green apparition of a meatball he had eaten for dinner. Writing that story opened a door to a world I got lost in. It was the first time I remember doing something where I truly forgot all about the real-life stuff happening around me, where I lost track of time and reality, and realized I could make *anything* happen—it was magic. The story ended badly for the poor boy, and though it had moments of humor, it was threaded through with bits of true darkness. My teacher, Mrs. Brennan, told me my haunted meatball story was good. She encouraged me to write more stories and bring them to her. So I went home each day after school, sat down at the dining room table with a Scooter Pie and glass of Hi-C, and wrote.

My next story was about a mud monster. Then there was one about orphans who lived in a haunted house. Another about a body buried behind the wall of a kid's bedroom that tapped messages to him at night. Creating these creepy tales made my little Monster Girl heart go pitter-patter. Of course, at the time, I didn't think about why I was drawn to write about the things that unsettled me, the terrible imaginings that kept me up at night. I didn't think about why I loved this stuff so much. As an adult who makes my living writing novels in which scary things happen—whether it's a serial killer or a vengeful ghost or a demonic possession—I've thought about it a lot.

Beyond the fictional horrors I sought out, there were a lot of real-world things that scared me. There was, of course, the ridicule and bullying I faced for being the odd girl out—the one who didn't dress right, didn't have a normal family, and brought creepy books to sleepovers. There was the growing terror I felt about the fact that I knew I liked girls and didn't dare tell a soul about it. And then there was my home life. My mother was an alcoholic who struggled with mental illness. I was never sure whom or what I might find when I got home from school each day: happy, manic mom who was ready to whisk me off on some adventure; morose, drunk mom who'd locked herself in her room; or, perhaps, unconscious mom with empty booze and/or pill bottles beside her. Or maybe she'd have disappeared without warning, and I'd have to wonder if this would be the time she didn't come back. My grandmother was an esteemed psychiatrist who did her very best to provide a safe and stable home for me and my little brother, but all her expertise and training couldn't seem to fix what was wrong with her own daughter. I'm sure I felt her fear, too. My brother was two years younger than me, and I desperately wanted to protect him from the chaos of our lives, but I was so often powerless to do so.

I realize now that watching, reading, and writing scary stuff helped me deal with all the things I found uncomfortable and terrifying about real life—it made me feel braver. It was horror I could control. If I got too scared, I could cover my eyes, turn off the TV, close the book, stop writing the story. And exploring my fears on the page helped me to learn things about myself. Maybe it even helped me build coping skills. And no matter how scared I got, there was always an immense rush at the end because I'd faced this terrible thing—the monsters, the darkness—on the page and survived. I was able to carry that bravery with me into the real world and maybe, just maybe, be a little less afraid. Not only less afraid, but better, stronger, more whole, and with a deeper understanding of myself and the world.

Now, all these years later, I've learned that I don't have to live out the dreams of nine-year-old me and go full-on werewolf to feel profound change. I just need to get lost in a horror novel, or to explore my fears by writing my own scary stories.

Horror has given me a place where I am not the perpetual outsider, the freaky Monster Girl; a place where I recognize myself in the monsters, the heroes, and everyone in between. We've all heard the writing advice: *Write what you know.* But my own take on that, my own writing mantra, is: *Write what scares you.* I've realized that to get to the truly good stuff, the stuff that gets my heart racing and mind whirling, I need to tap into my fears. When I drag them out from under the bed or from inside the closet into the light of day, I can explore them safely, poke at them with long sticks, ask my fears questions and learn truths about myself in the process. And now, just as when I wrote those first stories back in third grade, it makes me feel more brave. More alive.

On the Amtrak, Heading Home

By Josh Malerman

Josh Malerman burst onto the scene seemingly out of nowhere with his debut novel, Bird Box. *What no one knew about this member of the popular band the High Strung was that this novel was one of many he had fully written and stored in a trunk in his house. Malerman's work is hard to categorize, but I would argue that is also why he is so popular. Often setting his stories in his fictional universe of the neighboring towns of Goblin and Samhattan, Michigan, and always centering the uncanny, Malerman's individual works could be filed under horror, psychological suspense, science fiction, weird western, or even serial killer pigs (just to name a few). His ideas are so fresh and original that they capture readers' attention immediately. Then he goes on to reveal engaging and fully realized characters (both good and evil) and allows them to lead readers to places they never saw coming, making them fans for life.*

Malerman's essay represents an intermission of sorts, as we all take a step back from real-life horrors and supernatural monsters and, together, hop on a train from Chicago to Detroit. Trains in and of themselves have a rich history in fiction, as they are by definition a liminal space—they are the space between where the characters are and where they are going. In horror, the liminality of a train has been used throughout the genre's history to enhance the unease of a story. Malerman plays off this known trope and allows us to bear witness as he engages another passenger in a discussion about horror. Did this interaction actually happen? Maybe. Does it matter? No. Just sit back and enjoy the ride.

Readers new to Josh Malerman should start with Bird Box. *For those who want to try a similar author, I suggest Jonathan Janz.*

———

I noticed the academician before he noticed me. Maybe that's the writer in me.

He was a young man who would've been fresh-faced if not for the set furrowed brow above his light eyes—eyes I did not doubt had done a lot of reading, too. Some say birds of a feather spot one another the way vampires or drug addicts do, and maybe this is true, but I won't pat myself too hard on the back: the elbow patches of his clean tweed blazer and the stack of papers on his lap would've told anybody on the train he was a university man. But me, being who I am and considering what I love, I did wonder if perhaps his specific vocation was not books.

Turns out, it was. And while his idea of a life of letters varied from mine, the fact he was involved in any way placed the two of us in a duplicate, unseen train, two passengers traveling a literary world, a wondrous quiet bubble, within the wider, faster Amtrak carrying us from Chicago back home to Detroit. The Wolverine line was and is known for its knack of bringing transients together. But perhaps this is true of all trains.

I had a paperback copy of Robert Bloch's *Psycho II* peeled halfway open upon my knee; the young intellectual noted this before he glanced up to assess the man who held it, and I saw a brief, but sincere, blaze of confusion when he finally did lift his eyes to my own.

I knew then we'd talk. And I think, in hindsight, I knew even the specific content of the conversation we would have. Here sat a man who questioned why anybody, certainly someone wearing a suit like his own—that is, myself—would ever choose to read a book with such a horrid cover and uncouth title on a train, on a plane, or anywhere he considered sane. I, of course, continued to read, but with a sense of the young man, as his energy was difficult to ignore; it was clear to me he was building up either the courage or the verbiage to ask me a question, and the feeling was of a balloon growing fat with water from a hose until, eventually, it must pop.

"I say, friend," he said, his voice perhaps rockier than he would have liked it to have been, as the train hit a particularly pronounced bump just then. "What is that you're reading?"

As we weren't positioned directly across from each other, he had to lean in a bit to be heard. But as there was nobody in the seat facing mine, and me by the window, the decrease in distance between us almost came off as intimate.

"*Psycho II*," I said. "Same man who wrote the original. Robert Bloch. A funny man, too."

"Funny?" he said, incredulous. He shook his head, but I didn't think he'd end there. Too much energy between us already. "It seems to me that's a silly thing to spend any amount of time on."

"Oh? Go on."

"Well . . ." He adjusted the papers, setting them on the seat beside himself so he could lean farther yet. "You look like a serious man."

He gestured from my boots to my hat, as if this would make it clear I was, indeed, presenting a serious man.

"Hmm," I said. "I am. Sometimes. But not all that often. Are you so serious?"

He frowned. "I can tell you're being obtuse," he said. "Of course, neither of us are serious *all* the time. But when it comes to books, man . . . Yes. I'd think we're serious about what we choose to read, even if what we choose is meant to be humorous."

"Well, this particular book," I began, "is interesting, if only for being written as a follow-up to one of the greatest horror stories of our lifetimes."

Incredulity, again, on his young face. I smiled. I recognized something of my own early twenties in that face. Not quite dismissal. But close.

"Make me understand," he said, "how a man like you could spend his time reading . . . *horror* stories."

"I can do that."

"Enthusiastically, no less."

"With my full mind and body."

He leaned back in his seat just as the train hit another bump, somewhat propelling him forward once more. I gestured to the empty seat facing me.

"Let's give this talk a view," I said.

Beyond the murky train window, the industrial emptiness of northeastern Illinois—or was it northern Indiana?—traveled slow. I couldn't be sure we'd crossed the state line yet.

The young man got up, not without some agitation, and ducked beneath the cargo cases en route to the seat directly facing me. He was taller than I'd thought when he was still seated. Tall and thin. I thought of another Alfred Hitchcock adaptation: *Strangers on a Train*.

"Tim McCarthy," the man said, a little impatient, as though formalities were necessary now that we were face-to-face.

He extended his hand, and I shook it.

"Josh Malerman," I said. "And I don't only read it, I write it."

"Ah, see," he said, "I could tell you were a bookish man."

"That sounds like a long-haired, many-eyed creature."

"Ah, you're a funny person, aren't you?" He nodded to the book. "Is this why you read stuff of this nature? Psychos and . . . killers and what not?"

"Well, that just happens to be the book you happened to see me with. *This* book. Usually it's demons and ghosts. Psychopomps more than psychos."

"So, you're an occultist!"

"If only. I *wish*."

"Oh, come off it." Flustered now. "Have you nobody to introduce you to the classics?"

"I love it all. But wait. What classics are you referring to?"

"Lawrence! Woolf! Faulkner! Proust! Have you not read Marcel Proust?"

"I spent seven months with that man," I say. "Read all 4,347 pages of that book."

"Ah, I *knew* it." Pride now. Proud for having spotted a fellow big reader. "But that only makes this more confounding. How could someone who enjoys Proust, who has the stamina to read all of *À la recherche du temps perdu*, how can that man justify reading not only the source of one of the most violent films ever made, but the sequel no less?" He eyed the book. "I'm assuming *II* means this is, indeed, a lesser work, as sequels are sure to be."

"Well, yes. It's certainly not the original. *But* . . . now I know that fact, don't I? And taking the train home, I chose the company of an old friend. But here you are, and you may have eclipsed that need. And, assuming we end up in the bar car, I can close this little thing and put it in my pocket."

"Come on," he said. Shock now. "You read trash *and* drink?"

"Lots of both, yes."

"But do you have no respect for your intellect? I can't understand men like you." And henceforth came his reasoning: "I teach writing at Lansing Community College. It's a harrowing gig. I've seen so many young people with such potential all refuting their intellect. As if it were an act of rebellion. But it's one thing to defy your parents or the government."

"Indeed."

"But . . . your own potential? What are we . . . children? A man like you . . . why . . . you could read anything in the world that's ever been written. You could learn a new language. You could read Proust in the original *French*."

"That sounds like a lot of work."

"And does work frighten you? It does my students." The poor man. Racked with frustration. It was easy to imagine him standing before his class, longing for more.

"Do you have fun?" I asked.

"*Fun?*" He raised a finger as if to scold me, then paused, recognizing perhaps the ridiculousness in that. "Of course I have *fun*. Or I *could*, I suppose, if things went the way I believe they should."

"And which way is that?"

"Why, we should work hard. At our studies. To better ourselves. To grow. So many have forgotten the work it takes to stay in mental shape."

"I agree! We agree. You and me. And work *is* fun. Both can be true at the same time."

"I don't disagree."

"Settled then."

"But . . . *Psycho II*? You must give me a reason. I insist."

I realized here that I liked the young man. Fussy to a fault, perhaps. But was this such a bad thing?

A character, after all.

"When you say your students have turned their backs on their own minds . . . are you suggesting they ever had their intellects' best interest in mind?"

"Are you trying to fool me into a corner?"

"Are we debating?"

"Well, in a sense, yes. And *of course* my students once cared for their intellects. But in an unconscious way. *Childhood*, after all. Back when they were still ruled by instincts and not yet trends."

"Perfect you bring that up," I said. The train hit a big bump, and both of us rose from our seats before settling in again. "Childhood," I continued, "is the very reason I love horror the way I do."

"Come now, explain."

"Who is expected to believe in ghosts and ghouls, witches and warlocks, if not children?"

"But that's my point exactly. See?"

"I do. But it's mine, too. Think: if only there was a way to Trojan horse childhood into adulthood, to maintain that open-mindedness, that fascination with the weird, that wonder. You say children are ruled by instincts, and for this they instinctively protect their intellects, without perhaps knowing what that could possibly mean."

"Yes. But don't go saying the child's mind is superior."

"I'd never! Yet . . ."

"Yet?"

"If one were able to carry that belief, that *ability* to believe in ghosts, in demons, in vampires . . . if one could carry that essential exclusivity with them into their grown years . . ."

"Well, that all sounds healthy enough, to a point."

"Of course. There are subjects we're better off approaching purely as adults. Checkbooks, for example. But that doesn't mean there aren't subjects that could benefit from some of that childish wonder. Creativity, for one."

"Of course. But I don't imagine George Eliot prided herself on immaturity."

"I'm not so sure about that. I imagine Walt Whitman rather cherished a certain arrested development, a capacity to wonder, well into his later years. All the way, I'd say, till death did them part."

I arched my eyebrows and smiled, and he shook his head no.

"Are you so greedy for the morbid? All . . . demons and death?"

"In a way, yes. What fun subjects. But only because I *believe* in these things. I *believe* in the monster under the bed."

"You couldn't possibly . . ."

"For the duration of the work of art . . . I most magically do. And with the great works, I believe in it for many days after, too."

He made a funny face here. One I was happy to see. In it I saw the features of a young, strong-willed man who was open to ideas that differed from his own.

"So, according to you," he said, "that book there is something of . . ."

"A fountain of youth," I said. I held it up. "With this tome, and this genre, I am able to combine both forces, that of astute adult intelligence *and* childhood's grip on amazement. Think less of a time machine (or going back in time) and more of an overlapping of eras . . . ages . . . so that, while reading horror, one might live all the phases of life at once. Susceptibility, gullibility, and circumspection alike."

Tim McCarthy sat back and sighed. His eyebrows went up as the corners of his lips turned down. He slowly nodded, facing the window without seeming to look through the glass.

"Not bad," he said. "Not bad."

We hit another bump, and Tim and I both were pushed from our seats, so that we were leaning forward, eye to eye, when he said:

"But wait a minute, Malerman. There are other ways to do what you're suggesting. Magical realism, for example. Science fiction. There are *extraordinary* books that flirt with any number of subgenres, yet you've chosen horror."

"Chosen? Hmm. That's not the right word."

"What is the right word then, writer?"

I had to think on this. We both eased back into our seats as I did.

"I didn't *pick* horror, and I'm not going to sully this nice talk by simply reversing your statement and saying horror picked *me*. Rather, think of the genre itself as the imaginary friend you had (or did not have) as a child."

"I did indeed have one."

"Oh?"

"Yes." Here a bit of sun came through the window, and he had to squint. But I saw the mist of memory in his eyes. "He was a grown man, of all things." Tim laughed, a little self-conscious, but perhaps glad to think of this old friend once again. "A tall man who wore a red flannel shirt. I remember a black beard."

"Oh, and *I'm* the horror fan?"

"It's not like he carried an axe. No. He was a kind man. He pointed out the animals on my walks home from school. Squirrels and deer. Once a coyote."

"Did he tell you the names of the animals?"

"No. I don't think he ever spoke. But I understood he wanted me to witness these beasts in order to better myself. An enrichment, I suppose."

"Sounds like a good friend. What became of him?"

Tim laughed. "I grew up is what happened to him."

"Did you say goodbye as you grew up?"

"Of course not. One day I just simply stopped . . ."

Here Tim went quiet. Sadness fell softly upon his visage as though made of rice paper, descending uniformly by way of the air-conditioning of the Amtrak's Wolverine line.

"My God," he said. "I shouldn't feel as terrible as I suddenly do."

"You miss him."

"I didn't say goodbye. I didn't thank him." Then, "But what are you doing to me? You're an occultist after all, I see. A hypnotist of a sort. Of *course* I didn't say goodbye to my childhood imaginary friend. He never existed to begin with."

"But what is fiction then, if not imaginary friends? And don't you get so much out of books, so much that you'd feel drawn to a stranger on a train, to ask of him his preferences?"

Tim frowned the way people do when an opponent makes a decidedly wise move in a game of chess. But this wasn't a game to me. And I didn't want to win anything off this bright young man.

"Touché," he said. "But you *must* know that many in the literary set—nay, the world—might see, will *likely* see, horror as a subset of the greater medium—that is, the craft of writing a novel."

"Ooh, I like the sound of that," I said. "You're turning me into an outlaw. I rather enjoy the idea of working in a field that might be frowned upon or, say, overlooked in Oscar season."

"Ah!" Like he'd gotten me. Like he'd worked his way around that chess move of mine. "So, it *is* rebellion after all."

"You mentioned science fiction earlier. Magical realism. There are others, of course. But horror . . ." Here I felt something rise within me. A dark light, if such a thing can be. "The lights are dimmed with horror, the shadows greater. The imagination has more room, in this way, more space to play. In fact, because we can't see as far, we must *imagine* what lies farther out. Why would I assume it's one room when I might be standing in the foyer of an old decaying mansion? Or even the welcoming gate of an entire fictional town? This is where it becomes preference, I suppose. I prefer those shadows, that dim light; I like the lack of detail, color, even explanation. I feel infinite, facing that darkness. But that doesn't even compare to how it feels once you step *into* those shadows."

"Oh?" Tim said. He leaned forward. He looked something like a child then, and I imagined a grown man in a flannel shirt pointing me out to him. "Do tell . . ."

I looked both ways before speaking. The hum of the tracks ran beneath us like a held bass echo of a single bell.

"The deeper you go," I said, "the closer you come to the monsters and to the *possibility* of monsters, and with them comes the suggestion of other worlds, other planes of existence, including (but not exclusive to) an afterlife, a place where ghosts might be found. Fear, truly being afraid, puts you in a different place from where you currently sit. I *want* to be scared. I want the possibility it's all true. So, you see, to believe in ghosts for the duration of the read means to believe in *something* beyond death. And how much time do we spend in our books? And how much time then are we giving ourselves, *gifting* ourselves, with this outrageously optimistic point of view? *Horror*, Tim, is an optimistic thing. Because it suggests there is *more* to this life than what we know and what we accept as possible. And what is more optimistic than *more*?"

We sat silent then. I gripped the paperback on my knee once more and half expected him to return to his seat as he eyed the stack of papers still placed where he'd begun this trip.

"You make me want to read one of your books, Malerman," he said, with no resignation in his voice. Then, "I had not planned on any of you rubbing off on me, but here I am . . . considering these things."

"And you," I said, "have got me thinking seriously on a favorite subject of mine, a subject I wasn't planning on visiting today."

Tim smiled. "Perhaps that means we're a good team."

"I agree," I said. "And you know what good teams do after a victorious rout?"

"Do tell."

I gathered my things to rise. "They hit the bar car. Come."

I stepped into the aisle, and he gathered his papers and joined me there. We swayed with the easy motion of the Wolverine line.

"I live in Troy," he said, "but teach in Lansing. I'll take an Uber from Detroit, I suppose."

"Perfect," I said. "My fiancée, Allison, is picking me up in Detroit. And I try to keep a copy of a book in the car. I believe *Incidents Around the House* is in there now."

"Very well," he said. "It will be my first horror novel then."

I turned to him. "Do you mean to say you haven't read *any* horror?"

"Not even *Dracula*."

I smiled. "Oh my, do we have a lot to talk about up front. And the time to do it." We started walking, and I called back to him: "McCarthy? You were right."

"About what?"

"About me being something of an occultist. More of a magician, though."

"Really? Are you going to perform a prestidigitation for me?"

"Absolutely." We passed an elderly woman as we walked, a book open and on her lap. "And for my first trick, I will drink the first drink in half."

"Why do I feel you've told this joke before?" Then, "One more thing."

I faced him again in the aisle. "Why not many more things?"

"Is it really so spiritual for you? The way you describe it . . . a cherished arrested development, sneaking childhood into adulthood, the suggestion of an afterlife . . ."

"Let's not say 'spiritual,'" I said, "but '*spirited*.' Is there any story as vibrant as the horror story? From its flattest plains to its peaks, it's home. The horror story is home."

"Say, would you be interested in coming to my class? The students could use a slap of spirited."

"For real? Is this a real invite?"

"Of course. It's not every day people like us meet."

"I'm absolutely in," I said. Then, "Come on. I can't wait to hear what's home for you."

Tim smiled as we started up the aisle again. "By God," he said, "and I'm unexpectedly excited to tell you. In truth, at heart, I'm a realist."

"Oh no," I said. "We're going to need more drinks than I thought."

Why Horror?

By Paul Tremblay
Drawings by Emma Tremblay

Paul Tremblay is a perennial bestselling author whose books are held up as modern classics and mined for popular movies. His popularity is a direct result of how he writes: every one of his works will physically break you, but you will also be glad you have read them. Every. Single. Time. And it is on purpose, as he zeroes in on characters, placing them in a situation where a terrible truth is revealed. The hard part is next, for both him and the reader. How will he get them out of it? Will they survive? Can anyone live through this? Yes, there is violence in his stories, and because the danger and discomfort come from the characters, readers can easily see themselves in his stories, making them invested from the start and unable to extricate themselves. Finally, a Tremblay novel always has an ending that leaves the nature of the horror completely open-ended. He challenges readers to interpret the story as having either a completely rational or a supernatural explanation. The support for both opinions is there, and he will never divulge his personal opinion about it. Talk about unsettling!

Keeping with the interlude presented by Josh Malerman here in the middle of this book, the train we just rode on has left us at a new station, one with pictures. Tremblay uses his essay as a chance to contemplate the question "Why horror?" in a series of personal vignettes, illustrated by his daughter, Emma. From sharks to bees. From Jaws to Parker Brothers. Tremblay has a variety of answers to the question he poses in the title, and yet, they all lead to the same conclusion.

Readers new to Paul Tremblay should start with A Head Full of Ghosts. For those who want to try a similar author, I suggest Sarah Langan.

Why horror? My first memory: I was three years old, playing in the backyard of my grandparents' three-family house. My grandparents and an uncle lived on the first floor. My parents, my younger "Irish twin" sister, and I lived on the second floor, and an aunt and my older cousin lived on the third. It was a sunny fall day. My father was throwing me into a big pile of leaves, big enough that I sank over my head. After one of the tosses, I scrambled free from the leaf pile and looked down at my sweater-covered left arm. An apple-sized (to my eyes and memory) thing writhed under the wool. I don't remember the feeling of anything scrabbling against my skin, or maybe I choose not

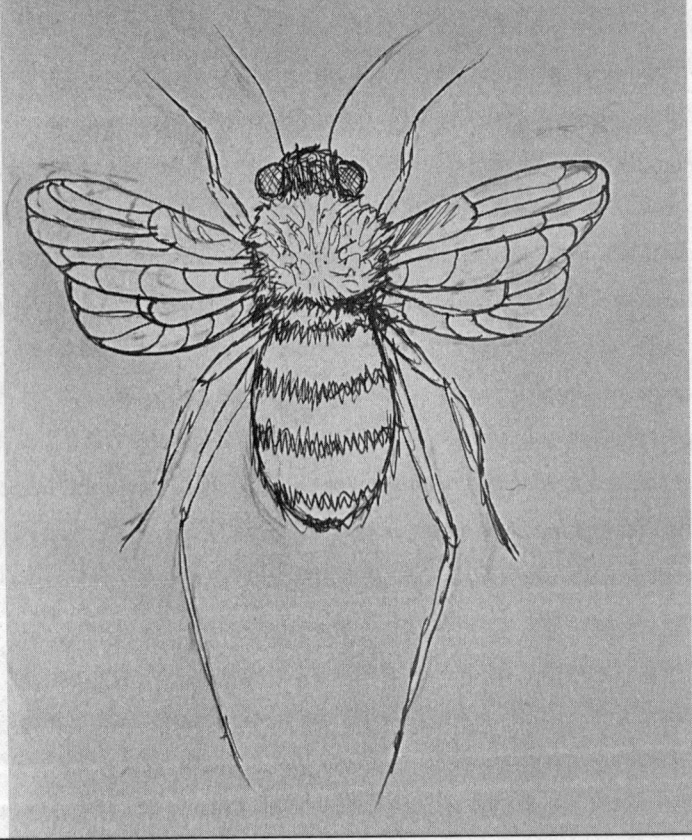

to remember. What I do remember is a squirming lump where there shouldn't have been one. I pushed my sleeve up and exposed a too-large, hairy, and brightly colored bee, and with the terrible truth of what was under my sweater revealed, it stung me. Later, I sat at the first-floor kitchen table, and I remember golden sunlight filtering in through partially shuttered windows. My grandmother tweezed out the stinger. As I cried and cooled my throbbing arm with an ice cube (I kept lifting the cube away to stare at the red dot on my puffy inner arm), someone in my family, I don't remember who, told me that the mean old bee would die now because it had stung me.

Why horror? I used to sleep with stuffed animals around my head to protect me from the monsters under my bed and in the closet or in the hallway or in the basement. I had my first nightmare (well, that's not accurate; it's my oldest nightmare, or the first one that I still vividly remember) when I was five years old. It happened not too long after we moved out of my grandparents' and into a 1,500-square-foot, three-bedroom, 1.5-bath Cape-style house on the other side of town. It's a house that I've used in my stories over and over again. The place was across the street from the Beverly School for the Deaf and one hundred feet away from perma-busy Elliott Street. There was no traffic light, and throughout childhood and my early teen years I risked life and limb to dash across Elliott Street, with the prize being the White Hen Pantry, where I bought baseball cards or candy as well as cigarettes for my mom. You could do that back then.

Shortly after moving into the new house, I dreamed that my father was sitting on the couch in the TV room. He had dark, almost black, shaggy hair and a thick beard. I was standing in the doorway between the TV room and the little-used living room. Without warning in the dream, he turned into a werewolf, or he *was* a werewolf. His transformation was instant, though I didn't see all of it. He didn't grow a snout. The dark hair grew and obscured everything on his face except for his teeth. I ran through the living room, and I ran so hard and fast that I smashed through the front windows, but he was right behind me, reaching and mingling with the broken wood and glass. I've had countless more nightmares, and even now as an adult, many of them end like that dad-werewolf one does, with an unexpected mad dash that ends on the precipice of me being caught.

Why horror? I saw *Jaws* on a big screen when I was ten years old. One summer my local high school hosted a screening in its auditorium. Dad pitched the movie to me by saying it included a scene that really captured the essence of fishing, of what it felt like when you first hooked a fish. We used to borrow Grampy's beat-up aluminum rowboat to catch flounder in Salem Harbor.

There was one time Dad, my sister, and I were out on the water, and a surprise storm rolled in. Fog enveloped us, and high winds turned the normally calm bay waters into chop and white-capped swells. My sister and I cheered Dad on, telling him that he was strong enough to row us to shore and beat the storm. Dad never let on how worried he was, even as the harbormaster happened by to tow us in. Years later, he admitted how scared he was out on that water because his frantic rowing wasn't moving the boat anywhere. It's the only time he's ever told me he was scared. Anyway, Dad was right about the scene where Quint first hooks the shark and how the slow, tentative tick of his reel was framed did replicate what I felt whenever a flounder nibbled on my line. But I was not prepared for what the rest of the movie would do to my brain, particularly Quint's death scene, when his screams cut out and he spits blood into the camera. I had shark nightmares for the better part of the following decade. That is not an exaggeration. Those shark dreams always ended mid-attack. There was one where the shark breached with me in its teeth and my vantage switched to that of an onlooker, though I knew it was still me flying through the air between the shark's teeth. I've watched *Jaws* more than fifty times, but I still cover my eyes during Quint's death scene. I've seen far gorier deaths in hundreds of other movies, but I'm afraid if I watch Quint spit blood again, my brain might revert to the one I had when I was ten.

Why horror? Like most people, I can't say that I enjoyed my adolescent years much, or at all.

I had a miserable time socially in middle and high school, as I was painfully skinny, had scoliosis, was acne-ridden, and was not confident and awkward with a capital *AWK*. I was lucky to have a roof over my head, though my parents (a factory worker and a bank teller) often and out loud worried about money. I was lucky to have a loving, local extended family, including a little brother with whom I shared a bedroom. He liked to watch monster movies, too. Though

that kid would soon outpace me, becoming a slasher/gore devotee. He first watched *The Texas Chain Saw Massacre* when he was ten. I didn't dare watch that movie until about ten or fifteen years ago. I still had frequent nightmares in my teen years, and yeah, some of them still featured sharks and monsters, but the scariest ones ended with the blinding flash of a nuclear bomb outside my bedroom window. I avoid books and movies about nuclear war because it's too scary, too disturbing. (I can't even include a mushroom cloud sketch here, so instead I asked Emma to draw a mushroom.)

After graduating high school I had surgery to correct my crooked spine, and I spent the summer before college recuperating and afraid of my basement, or extra afraid of my basement (it had always been a dark, dank, scary place), because of the first chapter of Stephen King's *It*. College was a far better experience for me socially than high school, and I discovered it was okay to be who I was or who I wanted to be and to like the things I liked. During college summers I worked with my dad at the Parker Brothers toy factory, which, nostalgic lens be damned, was a fun place to be. Everyone knew one another and everyone knew my dad, who was in the mailroom by the time I started working there. Horror fun fact: I helped mass-produce Ouija boards while there, which made me a little less afraid of them. Just a little.

One summer day in 1991, everyone in the factory was called to the lunchroom: assembly-line workers and mechanics, summer help, the execs and management, the truck drivers who shuttled between Salem and the warehouse in Danvers, and my dad. Without fanfare, some guy in a suit announced that Hasbro had bought Parker Brothers, and the factory was shutting down for good on November 1. All two-hundred-plus employees found out they were out of a job at the same time. There were cries and gasps and screams and angry shouts and open mouths and faces in hands. That mini nuclear bomb set off in the Parker Brothers lunchroom was the most horrific moment I've ever witnessed. I write about what being in that room felt like in nearly every one of my stories because I have to. There's something else I write about in nearly all my stories, too.

Why horror? I became a parent in late summer of 2000. My wife, Lisa—who had read King in her teens and bought me *The Stand* for my twenty-second birthday—could no longer watch or read horror after the birth of our son and then, four years later, our daughter. I went in the opposite direction. Filled with parental anxiety, I needed to watch and write and read horror. I needed stories about children and teens and parents in extremis. As a writer I needed to ask my characters (and myself and the reader), *What are you going to do now? How do you live through this? What happens when you're eventually, inevitably left alone?* while what was happening to them and around them, as well as the outcome, was unknown, was ambiguous and as murky as a darkened

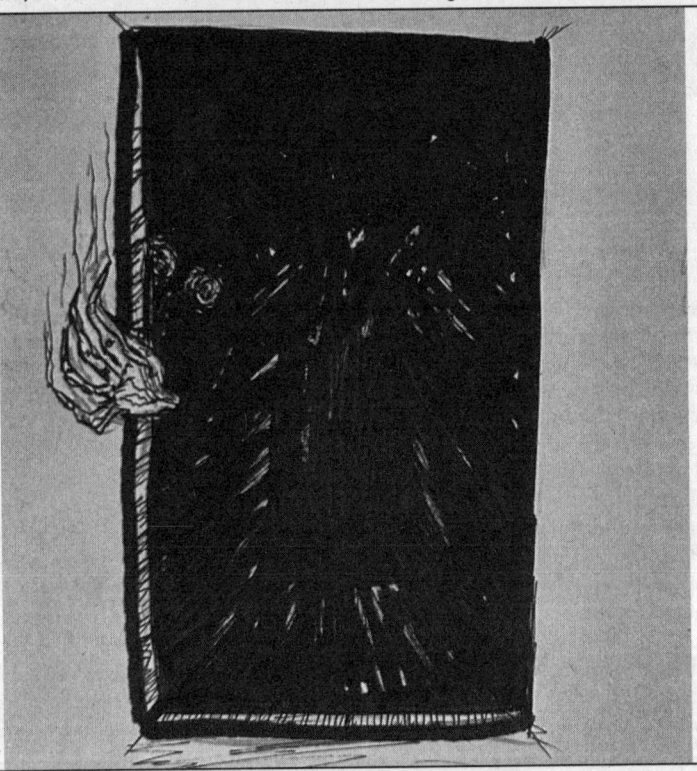

room. And yeah, the other thing I'm always writing about is being alone in a dark room, which on its surface is an obvious metaphor for being afraid of dying. But there's more to it, I think, just as there's more to horror. Monsters are cool, and the awe of horror, the wonder and possibility it presents, is an undeniable appeal to both the adult-me and the kid-me I keep locked inside my chest. But I need horror because, when done well, horror communicates simple and complex truths. Terrible truths, yes, but as a reader and moviegoer, I find comfort and hope that the authors and filmmakers recognize there's something terribly wrong, and that they feel like I do. That shared recognition makes me feel less like I'm sitting alone in a dark room, or it makes that dark room waiting at the end of the hallway seem a bit farther away.

Why I
Love Horror

By Grady Hendrix

Grady Hendrix began his career as a horror novelist leaning into parody and humor, but over the years, while he has found ways to continue to incorporate humor, his novels have gotten progressively more serious and darker. Hendrix's stories feature a strong, often nostalgic sense of place and even stronger female protagonists overcoming dangerous, supernatural events that arise from what readers can easily identify as mundane situations. Another interesting quirk about Hendrix is his insistence on not being pigeonholed. He has stated many times that he goes out of his way to make sure every novel examines a new horror subgenre or trope, thus introducing his legions of fans to the full breadth of the genre's offerings. Finally, Hendrix is also a proud historian of the 1970s and '80s era of pulp horror, as demonstrated in his Bram Stoker Award–winning nonfiction survey of the era, Paperbacks from Hell.

Like Paul Tremblay, Hendrix also has a personal reason for his deep love of horror; however, unlike Tremblay's lighter tone, Hendrix shares a dark story about his father, someone Hendrix does not often write about. This essay also begins a theme seen in the following three essays, all of which deal with trauma and how horror helped to process it. I greatly appreciate the authors who have shared their difficult, personal stories here, because sometimes the road to horror runs right through your most intimate experiences. Please know that if these essays' discussion of very real trauma is too much for you, you can skip to Rachel Harrison's essay.

Readers new to Grady Hendrix should start with The Southern Book

Club's Guide to Slaying Vampires. *For those who want to try a similar author, I suggest Daniel Kraus.*

———

I opened my dad's freezer and found a child's severed arm.

Behind me, Amy Jordan said, "Is there a frozen pizza or something?"

The arm had been cut off mid-biceps, and the raw tufted meat had frozen into a livid red scream against its gray skin.

"Or we could have sardines?" Amy opened another cabinet. "Jesus, what's up with your dad and sardines?"

My family had ignored a secret stash of canned meat in the back of a kitchen cabinet for years, and then, when my dad moved out, for some reason he took every last, dusty one of them: Spam, clams in tomato sauce, anchovies, deviled ham. Sardines. They were the only actual food Amy and I had found when we started searching his beach house kitchen for breakfast. I mean, besides a black banana on the counter and half a jar of crunchy peanut butter he kept in the fridge.

Then I'd opened the freezer.

Amy and I always wound up together because she and her mom had moved in around the corner last year and we went to the same school. We weren't best friends, but we were always giving each other rides, and that week we'd been out at Wallace Stoney's graduation party at his parents' beach house. We were juniors, but our school was grades one through twelve and the classes were small, so we'd all known one another forever. Wallace's parents let him take over their beach house on Kiawah for a week, and seventy of us had been out there for days smoking Southern

Magic (which was supposed to get you high but never did) and funneling Coors Light in the dunes. At night everyone who wasn't hooking up in the beds passed out on the floors, and it all started over again in the morning.

I'd slept under a beach towel in a deck chair out back and woke up with the sun. I'd gone into the kitchen and found Amy opening and closing empty Domino's boxes. We were tired and sandy and had headaches, so we decided to take off in my van before anyone woke up.

When my dad moved out he'd lived in a couple of clinically depressed apartments before realizing he was paying taxes on a perfectly good beach house out on Seabrook Island, so he packed up his clothes and his sardines and moved in. Seabrook was right next door to Kiawah, and it was 8:00 a.m. on a Saturday morning, which meant my dad would already be at the hospital, so I told Amy we could stop there to shower and get breakfast. It was too early for anything to be open except gas stations, and it was a long drive back into town.

"There's Bisquick," Amy said, opening the cabinet over the stove. "And a can of PAM."

My dad had wrapped the child's arm in Saran wrap that was peeling loose, and now it lay over it like a sci-fi shroud. Its fingernails were blue and its fingers had curled into its palm. This frozen monkey paw rested on top of a Lean Cuisine (linguine with clam sauce).

"Why does your dad keep his peanut butter in the fridge?" Amy asked.

I don't know. Why does he keep a child's arm in the freezer?

Years later, Jim Jameson would get caught with a child's severed foot in a crab trap. A tropical storm had come through Charleston and washed it up on Folly Beach, and the police started asking questions about, you know, a child's severed foot in a crab trap, and Jim Jameson came forward and said it was his. He told them he was an orthopedic surgeon and the foot possessed an interesting bone deformity. After he'd amputated it, he'd asked the parents if he could keep it to use as a teaching tool. They'd said yes, and apparently the best way to get the meat off its bones was to let the crabs strip it.

When I read this in the paper I called Amy, because we'd gone to high school with Chrissy Jameson, Jim's daughter.

"You know what they did after he said that?" Amy asked. "They gave it back to him."

I never asked Chrissy about it because we didn't really keep up. I'd had such a crush on her, though. She was soft-spoken and beautiful and super into art, and after we went to prom together everyone headed out to her grandmother's place in Meggett. Her grandmother had been dead forever and no one had touched a thing in that house. Even the cans in the kitchen were from the '70s.

After a lot of Coors Light and a bit of Southern Magic, Chrissy asked me if I wanted to see something, and she took me into the big bedroom and I thought for sure we were going to hook up because we were standing right next to the bed, but instead she opened a drawer full of human hair. From back to front, from one side to the other, the drawer overflowed with hair, shading from dark brown to light gray.

"It's my grandmother's," Chrissy said. "From her brush. She saved it all her life. She thought throwing part of herself away was wrong."

We didn't hook up that night.

The following year, her mom divorced her dad and moved out to the Meggett house and turned it into an ostrich ranch. Five years after that, Jim Jameson was putting a child's severed foot in a crab trap.

When I came home from New York that year I had Thanksgiving with my dad at his favorite restaurant, a hibachi place called Chow's Steakhouse on Highway 17. While the chef turned a stack of onion slices into a volcano on the grill, I asked my dad about Jim Jameson's foot.

"Isn't it unethical or something?"

"Crabs are the best way to get the meat off the bone," my dad said. "Everyone's making a fuss over nothing."

I pointed out that people ate crab out of the harbor, and there was now a greater than zero chance that the crab they were eating had eaten human flesh. My dad shrugged.

"You never ate a scab?"

Suddenly, I was overwhelmed with an urge to ask him about the arm. Because my dad wasn't an orthopedic surgeon, he was a cardiologist, and there was nothing he could teach his students with a child's severed arm. Just then, the chef catapulted a shrimp into the mouth of the little girl sitting beside us, and the whole table burst into applause.

"You know what'd happen if that got lodged in her trachea?" my dad asked.

I didn't answer, because he was already pulling a ballpoint pen out of his shirt pocket.

"I'd lay her down on the floor and take this pen and jam it through her windpipe, right below her trachea. Then I'd pull out the ink cartridge and blow down it and give her mouth to mouth through the hollow body of this pen until the EMS arrived."

My dad loved the idea of performing emergency surgery. When we were on an airplane and the captain asked if there were any doctors on board, my dad hit his call button like he was on *Family Feud*. When I was a kid we'd gone to the ballet, and halfway through the first act someone in the front row started hollering if there was a doctor in the house, and my dad practically hurdled the rows to get to them. Turned out they'd only fainted. No one could cheer him up after that, and we left at intermission.

I could never figure out if his urge to perform emergency surgery was because he loved the rush or because he wanted us to see what he did for a living.

I saw what he did for a living. Once.

We'd taken my sister to college outside Boston and were walking back across the parking lot after dinner when we heard that sickening hollow boom of a car hitting another car. Even if you've never heard that sound before, you instantly know what it is. We all stopped and looked over at the dark stretch of road at the far end of the lot. It was on a blind corner, and as we watched, another car flew around it and slammed into the two wrecked cars. Then another. Then another. There was a pause, then from far away we saw a big pickup truck coming, way over the speed limit, and people on the street started shouting at the guy to stop, but he didn't hear. He plowed into that five-car pileup at full speed. There was silence for a moment, then the people trapped in the cars started to scream.

My dad ran like he was coming off the starting blocks at the four-hundred-yard dash, cardiologist division, leaving my mom and me behind. He came back to the hotel room after eleven that night, covered in blood. It was smeared up to his elbows, it was slathered across his knuckles and neck, it stained his pants. There was half a handprint on the chest of his shirt.

It was the first time I ever saw my dad covered in blood.

It wouldn't be the last.

Because of his emergency surgery obsession, I always assumed that's what doctors did. So when I was going through my whole "I'd rather live with Dad" phase and staying out at the beach house with him one sum-mer, I never thought it was weird when he came home late from work with blood smeared across the face of his watch or flecked on his collar. I always assumed a lot of random people needed help.

One night, he called to tell me he'd be really late and not to stay up. I made a frozen pizza, watched MTV, then went to bed in the loft that looked down on the living room. I woke up when the front door opened. My dad wore an apron of blood, from his eyebrows to his ankles. He care-fully took off his shoes and walked straight to his bedroom. A few sec-onds later, I heard the shower. It was still running when I fell back to sleep.

I asked him about it in the morning.

"A farmer hit a deer," he said. "I found him pulled over on Bohicket Road acting funny. I made sure he didn't have a concussion, then helped him get the deer off his car. He stunk like a brewery."

This is what doctors did for a living, right?

To the day he died, my dad had no idea what I did for a living. A friend of mine from high school ran into him at the hospital after he retired and asked him what I was up to these days.

"Import-export," my dad said. "He imports little toys from Asia and sells them."

My friend said they'd heard I was a horror writer. No, my dad said, Asian toys. Then he shook his head.

"Grady? A horror writer?" He laughed. "He's too scared to write those kinds of books."

My dad had decided I was too scared after what happened that time with his mother. Granny had moved in with us when she was in her late seventies and probably had Alzheimer's, although back then we all just thought, you know, old people got funny sometimes.

Everyone told me I loved Granny when I was little. I wish I could remember that, because by the time she came to live with us I couldn't stand to look at her. Years later, I'd try to apologize by writing her into my book *The Southern Book Club's Guide to Slaying Vampires*. I wanted to give her a hero moment that she never got at the end of her life. But when she lived with us, I didn't even want to be in the same room with her.

She couldn't keep food in her mouth, and my mom insisted she eat with us at the table. Clumps of chewed food stuck to her glass in a mushy crust or dissolved at the bottom of her apple juice; her hands shook so hard she dropped most of what she tried to eat down her housecoat. She talked to people who weren't there and smelled like adult diapers, and when she got angry or frustrated, which was all the time, she'd pinch you so hard she left bruises.

I wasn't scared of her, though, until that night when I was ten. My parents were going to a party at a neighbor's and said they'd be back early. Granny was already sitting up in her chair dressed for bed, and all I had to do was take her dinner tray when she was finished and they'd put her to bed when they got back.

Even at ten years old I knew I was getting a raw deal, but they never went anywhere together because my dad was always at the hospital, so I didn't feel like I could say no. Right after they left, it started to rain. The rain turned into a storm fast, and sheet lightning flickered out over the harbor while thunder shook the roof. Rain lashed the windows. The power dimmed, then came back strong. I stayed in the den with the TV and decided I'd leave Granny's tray until my mom and dad got back.

Then Granny started rapping her knuckles on her tray.

Whenever Granny wanted something she'd start knocking on a table or her tray or the arms of her rocking chair, over and over again, until you finally went and asked her what she wanted. She wouldn't pause, she wouldn't stop, just the same monotonous knocking until you finally gave in. And here she was, knocking away upstairs in that dark house.

I ignored her for as long as I could, but she went on and on, knocking her swollen knuckles against her metal tray again and again, until finally I went upstairs and stood in her door and said, "What do you want, Granny?"

She stopped knocking. She sat hunched over, moaning low like she was in pain, but that's what she always did. I started breathing through my mouth, went over, leaned down, grabbed her tray, and she grabbed me.

She hooked my shirt with two clawed fingers and I tried to pull away, but she was strong and she held me there and said in my ear, "I know where Grady goes. I know where Grady goes. At night. I know where Grady goes. I know where Grady goes at night. I know where Grady goes. I know where Grady goes at night."

She kept croaking that and I didn't want to hear it and I yanked myself away, hard, and her finger ripped a button off my shirt. Then I was backing across the room while she stared at me with her pale, blurry eyes leaking tears, dripping off her chin, saying, "I know where Grady goes. I know where Grady goes. At night."

My dad and I, we're both named Grady.

I locked myself in the Volvo out in the driveway until my parents got home.

They had a fight later on, and through their closed bedroom door I heard my dad say, "I didn't know he was such a scaredy-cat. What makes him that way?"

"Your dad is weird," Amy Jordan had said the minute we came into his Seabrook house. He had the dining room table buried under a pile of photo store envelopes overflowing with snapshots, and while I had the first shower, Amy went through them. When I came out she said, "These are a cry for help."

She didn't get my dad. He loved taking pictures but he was terrible at it. He took pictures of the backs of people's heads, of beautiful landscapes from angles that made them look boring, of random objects, of my sisters and me, never smiling.

Every time we stayed at a hotel, he'd set the camera on the dresser and put on the timer, then we'd have to sit on the bed and take a family portrait. After my parents got divorced he would do it with just himself and mail me the pictures.

"In Texas," he'd write on the back of a snapshot of him smiling in a chair in an empty hotel room. "At a conference in Michigan."

Then his camera broke and he got one that didn't have a timer so he couldn't take pictures of himself anymore. That's when he started mailing me pictures of empty hotel rooms.

"Orlando, Florida," he'd write on the back of them. "Palm Springs, California. At a conference."

He traveled to a lot of conferences, and my collection of empty hotel room photographs grew. I always dreaded opening the envelopes, because my dad wasn't careful.

When I graduated from NYU, my mom and dad both came up to attend the ceremony and they were perfectly civil. They stayed in separate hotels, but that was it. I moved back home for the summer and came home one day to find a plastic Harris Teeter bag hanging on my mom's front doorknob with the pictures my dad took at graduation. He'd put a note in the bag that said "Tell me if you want any duplicates. Love, Dad."

I went through them: A picture of the twenty-four-hour parking lot on Astor Place where we'd never parked. The backs of people's heads in caps and gowns. A street full of people I didn't know. Five pictures of an empty hotel room. He'd stayed at the Ramada Renaissance, and from the pictures I could tell he'd gotten himself a suite.

The room was dark and he was using his flash so everything looked flat and high contrast. And I noticed a shape on his bed, a long one, covered up with a blanket. I looked closer and realized it was a person with a blanket pulled all the way over their head. The only thing that stuck out from under the blanket was an arm. I think it was a woman's arm because she had on a thin gold watch. Her fingers were curled over into her palm, like a child's arm in a freezer.

It made me think about dead-arming. Franco Cobb had told everyone in seventh grade that you could dunk your arm in a cooler of ice up to your shoulder and then touch people with it. It was numb and felt like a corpse. Everyone did it until Greg Altman pointed out that Franco probably did it to jerk off. After that we called him Necro instead of Franco. A seventh grader can't survive a nickname like Necro Cobb. He transferred out before the end of the year.

I looked at that picture of a woman covered by a blanket in my dad's hotel room, her arm sticking out, and that's the first thing I thought about: Necro Cobb and dead-arming.

Every now and then someone asks me to write an essay or give an interview about "why I love horror" and I never do. I turn them down casually, saying, "It's just what I do." I deflect. I redirect. I take the interview in another direction.

Back in first grade, Mrs. Rhett drove carpool, and in an attempt to control a bunch of six-year-old boys she told us ghost stories. Some were jokes with punch lines like "Then she took a cough drop and the coffin disappeared"; others were classics like "The Golden Arm" and the one about the girl who sticks a cane through her dress in a cemetery and thinks it's a dead person grabbing her skirts and has a heart attack and dies. Mrs. Rhett set the stories in places we knew and used names we'd heard before, and at the end of every single one of these dusty old chestnuts we'd all ask, "Is it true?" and she'd wait until she pulled up at drop-off before answering with the scariest word in horror: "Maybe."

I love horror because it's the one genre that claims to be true. All the way back to Horace Walpole's *The Castle of Otranto* in 1764, horror stories are supposed to be something that really happened to someone— a story found in a bundle of old letters or in a lost diary, brittle with age. From *The Turn of the Screw* to *The Blair Witch Project*, they're all supposed to make you wonder if they really happened. Only horror does that. There's no such thing as a found footage rom-com.

Horror is the genre that's supposed to make you think, *Did this really happen? Is the world stranger and more dangerous than I thought? Who are these people I live with? What's really going on inside their heads?*

The reason I agreed to write this essay is because I published a book called *How to Sell a Haunted House* about two kids dealing with the death of their parents, and a few months later my dad died. I sat with him all week as he went and the skin melted from his skull until he looked just like his mother, moaning like he was in pain, arms tucked under the covers, blanket pulled up to his chin, eyes reading the ceiling. And as I sat with him I thought about where Grady went at night, and what Granny knew, and what I'd found in his freezer that morning.

So maybe this is true, what I'm writing here. Or maybe it's not. Maybe it's just enough truth to sell the parts that aren't. Maybe that arm in the freezer stands for some other secret my dad kept that I could sense the shape of but never quite pin down. Or maybe that arm really was there, along with all the other things a child's severed arm implies: a shoulder, an amputation, a child.

I think you know what I mean.

You see your dad come home bloody a few times, but maybe he was helping a farmer who hit a deer, and maybe that photo was just something between him and a woman in New York City who humored his weird request, and maybe his mother said she knew where he went at night and it made her cry because she had Alzheimer's, and maybe that arm was just a teaching tool for someone he knew in orthopedics.

Maybe.

But in 1990, Amy Jordan and I stood in the kitchen of my dad's beach house and I opened the freezer and found a child's severed arm barely covered in Saran wrap and I didn't say a word. Under its palm was a Lean Cuisine linguine with clam sauce and under its raw hamburger stump was a box of French bread pizza, and I pulled the pizza out and closed the door and put it in the microwave for six minutes on high and served it to Amy.

I had the sardines.

I told her I wasn't hungry.

Maybe I had some of the pizza? Honestly, it was thirty-something years ago. I can't remember anymore. What I do remember is that I dried the towels we used and folded them up very carefully before putting them back on the shelf, and I took the pizza box with us and threw it away in a McDonald's dumpster. I was very careful not to leave any trace of us behind. I didn't want my dad to know we'd been in his lair.

I wasn't scared of my dad, but that day I realized I didn't know him. He was a stranger to me. Whatever was going on behind his eyes, I didn't have a clue. We slept in a house with a man we didn't know, we let our guard down around him for years, and when we saw something that didn't fit the story of our family, we made it go away.

That scares me. That scares me a lot.

Is this story true? Like Mrs. Rhett said, maybe.

Maybe that arm was in my dad's freezer. Maybe it wasn't. Maybe you understand what I'm talking about, or maybe this is something you can't possibly understand. Maybe your family's too different from mine. Maybe you've never seen something that didn't fit, or if you did, maybe you made it go away. Maybe this is something just between us Gradys.

Maybe.

But I'm pretty sure I had the sardines.

And that's why I love horror.

My Mother Was Margaret White

By Cynthia Pelayo

Cynthia Pelayo is a critically acclaimed poet, journalist, and novelist. Her work looks to fairy tales and fables of yore for inspiration, all of which hold a serious darkness that she uses to her advantage as she juxtaposes these well-known stories with very real horrors, often focused on murder. Pelayo's writing style is engaging and vivid. She takes readers by the hand and leads them through stories that fascinate and frighten, tales filled with as much love as anguish, conjuring a sense of awe to battle the darkness, and all of it featuring sympathetic, but complicated, characters. It is important to note that Pelayo's thriller-horror hybrids are also always set in her hometown of Chicago, and her deep affection for the place, warts and all, always shines through.

Pelayo's essay continues the theme of parental trauma as she addresses in clear and direct language the serious trauma she endured at the hands of her mother, how every day she must process it, and how being a consumer of horror is one of the things that gave her the framework she needed to not only live but also thrive. Please note, Pelayo included this trigger warning for all readers: "The following essay mentions childhood abuse, suicidal ideation, and self-harm."

Readers new to Cynthia Pelayo should start with Forgotten Sisters. *For those who want to try a similar author, I suggest Gwendolyn Kiste.*

My philosophical views are aligned with Stoicism, an ancient Greek and Roman philosophy popularized by Seneca, Epictetus, and the

Roman emperor Marcus Aurelius. It's their teachings and those of other spiritual leaders, as well as lessons I have learned in being a consumer of horror, that have helped me process the traumas of life.

Each morning I usually read a Stoic teaching, followed by text from another spiritual teacher. I then journal, writing three pages of stream of consciousness—"morning pages," they are called, popularized from *The Artist's Way* by Julia Cameron—and a list of affirmations and items I'm grateful for and recite those. I then proceed with a series of EFT (Emotional Freedom Technique) tapping, which is a method based on acupressure that was developed in the 1990s to help ease PTSD in veterans. Then I meditate anywhere from a half an hour to an hour. These are the bulk of the methods I employ to manage my CPTSD, anxiety, panic disorder, agoraphobia, and more.

The Stoics say that virtue is enough to succeed, and while this may be in conflict with others' worldview (and I accept that), this is my belief and the tenets that I have held true to my life. This philosophy, along with my other belief systems, has helped to ground me throughout a number of challenging life moments, being a first-generation Puerto Rican woman to grow up on the mainland.

My parents were raised in rural Puerto Rico in the 1940s. My mother grew up in a conservative Catholic household on a farm, and my father grew up in a much more liberal Pentecostal home in the mountains. Both of them held only sixth-grade educations, worked in factories throughout their lives, and eventually made their way to Chicago, where they met and married in the 1970s.

My mother is emotionally stunted, and while she's nearly in her eighties, she is very much still like a little girl. We attribute this to the severe beatings she received as a young girl from her father that equate to torture: being forced to kneel on raw grains of rice in the hot sun for hours, for example. Unfortunately for me, my mother was not mentally equipped to raise children, and so she repeated the pattern she was raised in, beating me mercilessly until I was twenty-one.

It sounds shocking to think of that today, to say I lived in that house for so long, but back then, there was no internet, there was no social media, there was no way out. And so most of my life in that house was spent in my ten-by-twelve bedroom, often afraid to leave that room, because if I encountered my mother in a mood, and she very often was in a mood, I would get slapped, hit with an electrical cord, hit with her shoes, my hair pulled, pushed down the stairs, or more. I was once beaten so bad I could not go to school for a week because of the bruising.

School wasn't much better. I was bullied there as well. I was a socially awkward child, and I was not allowed to make friends. I was not allowed to attend birthday parties or even talk on the phone. I was not allowed to play outside. I was not allowed to talk to people, to connect with people. I was not allowed to exist beyond that bedroom and that house.

The very first horror movie I saw was *A Nightmare on Elm Street*. My oldest brother was babysitting me. It must have been 1985 or 1986. I walked into the living room, and on the old wooden floor television set I see this man covered in shadows extend his arms across an alley; his fingers are knives scraping against a surface with a high-pitched screech. I screamed, and my brother paused the VCR and told me it was all right, that I was safe, that the monster in the television could not hurt me, and it was at that moment I became transfixed. Here was this very real, scary thing and I could face it, I could finally face this scary something and, no matter what, it could not hurt me.

It was at that moment I became a horror fan.

I would spend a lot of time poring through *TV Guide*, searching for horror film listings, staying up late to watch *Alfred Hitchcock Presents*, *The Outer Limits*, *Tales from the Darkside*, *The Twilight Zone*, and more. My father was completely fascinated by my interest in horror, and he would stay up late with me too, watching scary movies and encouraging my love of it. My mother was not happy with my love of the genre, even going so far as to call our family priest to the house to tell me that horror was bad and horror would allow the Devil in and that horror would destroy my life.

Horror has instead saved my life.

The very first time I watched *Carrie* I felt like I was her, Carrie, bullied at school, tormented at home. My mother didn't have a prayer closet like Margaret White; she instead had an altar in the living room with a three-foot-tall statue of Jesus. My bedroom door faced it, so when I'd open it, sometimes I'd see my mother there, kneeling in front of her altar, red and white wax candles flickering, her hands folded in prayer. It was terrifying. My mother talked about Jesus like he was an actual person watching me and hovering over me at all times. She told me everything I did offended her and him. She told me I was ugly. She told me I was too skinny. She told me I was too fat. She called me a whore when I wore too-tight shirts, and then she responded further by ripping up all my clothes and throwing them in the trash. My mother cursed me and told me she prayed I'd have children who would make me suffer as much as I had made her suffer. After I drank a bottle of pills to just quiet it all, she told me that the emergency room bill was so astronomical that I should have just died.

I would pray to God a lot in those years, asking Jesus why he hated me so much, why my mother hated me, why the kids and teachers at school did too. I remember so many nights crying myself to sleep. I once had a dream of that three-foot-tall Jesus statue entering my room at night; he didn't say anything, just moaned in pain.

I very much sympathized with Carrie. I was her. I am her. Someone who grew up in a quiet home, who was a little too naive and gullible, who had been taken advantage of because of being too emotionally stunted from abuse and being raised in a strict Christian conservative home.

I didn't have many people to reach out and talk to at that time. In the 1980s and 1990s, everyone knew I was being severely beaten at home—the kids and adults in the neighborhood, students and teachers. Everyone knew and no one did anything, they only just ever laughed, just like they laughed at Carrie.

My only salvation in that house was my dad, whom my mother abused as well. She'd scream at him and scratch him until he bled and hit him with things—pots and pans, anything. Sometimes I'd run to him, my arms out as she was hitting him, begging her not to hurt my daddy anymore. I asked my dad once why we didn't call and get her help, but he responded with "She's my wife, what am I supposed to do?" I can only think now my father was just scared, scared of her being institutionalized, or her becoming further lost to her own rage and into her own mind. Still, we all suffered so much because of her.

Eventually, my father bought me a small television and a VCR, and he'd take me to the neighborhood video rental store and tell me I could rent whatever I wanted. I went down the entire section of horror films and rented each and every one throughout that time, watching the entire *Nightmare on Elm Street* series, *Friday the 13th*, *Halloween*. I was watching *Hellraiser* at nine, *Faces of Death* by ten, *The Last House on the Left* by twelve, *The Texas Chain Saw Massacre*, all of it. I watched all of it. I watched whatever I could find, whatever I could get my hands on, and whatever could make me feel that, yes, there are monsters out there, and no matter how much they try to break me down and break me apart, I can still fight back, I can still control my mind and my thoughts, and they can never have that.

In those years, I didn't really have any friends, or anyone. If someone wanted to befriend me, if they called my house and my mother answered, she would say, "Cynthia? She's dead," and hang up the phone. Everyone knew what my mother was like and everyone was frightened of her, and so everyone stayed away from me. After high school, my choice was the military, as we were a military family, and then I was going to go to the convent right after, anything to get out.

Unfortunately, I was medically discharged from the army for scoliosis, a condition I didn't even know I had until then, and when I came back home I was desperately afraid I would not survive much longer in her home, but my now husband saved me.

I was allowed to leave if I got married, and I married my best friend, who promised me he'd protect me and wouldn't allow anyone to ever abuse me or hit me ever again. He's protected me significantly over the years, but it's life, and we can't be protected from everything. I struggle now with physical touch and sometimes it's difficult to hug my own children. I've tried talk therapy, but I don't like to talk about these things, and it only stirs it all up to the surface. When the emotions get stirred up it can take me days or weeks or months to shake those memories; to shake the image of my mother standing over me, choking me; to shake the rumors the middle school kids spread around the school about me that contributed to me being attacked by a classmate. There's just so much, and I muffled and muted it all with those monsters on my television who saved me from it all.

Horror also helped me process a series of traumatic miscarriages I had years ago. After we lost a baby at five months, I came home from the hospital and played the French extremism film *Inside*, about a woman whose baby is ripped from her body by an unknown assailant. After that film, I sat in my dark living room and cried, knowing that my baby too was in a way ripped away from me. There was something about watching the brutality of those scenes that helped me process my anger, my disappointment, and the weight of all that I was experiencing emotionally.

I've attempted suicide three times in my life, once at sixteen, once after that traumatic miscarriage, and again after the death of my father. At sixteen, I was just overwhelmed by my mother and her abuse; after the miscarriage, I was just so physically and emotionally broken I could not see how I could continue; and after my father, well, I could not imagine living another forty years without him to protect me from the world. Shortly after his death, I once again was up against a weight of criticism and rumors and mockery in my life. He'd always protected me, and now that he wasn't here, I felt that much more exposed to the horrors of reality and alone. Yet, I think I've been able to push through because before he died he begged my husband, whom he loved very much, to continue taking care of me and protecting me. Also, because on my father's deathbed he turned to me and told me, "Keep writing your stories. That's all you need to do to keep safe." And so I always turn to that thought when the emotions grow so big that I just need to write through these monsters, through all these awful things to get to the light.

I grew up in an abusive household with an abusive mother, and here in my mid-forties, I am still dealing with the effects from her emotional and physical abuse. And while forgiving one's abusers is a personal choice,

I have decided to forgive my mother. She has received some treatment and begged for my forgiveness, and I acknowledge too that she was never equipped with proper emotional tools. She was never loved nor given the freedom to just be a child herself. When I watch her spend time with my children today, sometimes I have to leave the room and cry because I am overwhelmed with how gentle and kind she is with them, and I wish that I had a mother like that when I was a little girl.

But this, all of it, is what makes me a horror writer, I suppose. This, all of it, is why I love horror, because so many of these fictional stories and films have communicated to me that there is a glimmer of beauty somewhere in this night, and there is a speck of hope somewhere in all this grief and suffering, and somewhere within the screams and brutal blows there is salvation. Horror, particularly the horror I favor, teaches me that there is an end, and that there is peace, and that there will be a morning after the darkness.

Sometimes I sit in my office at home for up to fourteen hours a day. It's a small room, about six by twelve, the former back porch we enclosed. It's painted white with two big windows that look out into the backyard. My bookshelves are full, and so I had to purchase some book carts and now those are full, and so now there are books stacked on the floor, but still, I feel safe and calm here, surrounded by my books, horror novels, fairy tales, poetry, and more. As I've grown older my anxiety and agoraphobia have only increased, so I cling to this small room packed with stories like I clung to my small room when I was a little girl and I remind myself that I am safe here. When I step outside of here, that tension grows, because I know that outside there in the world anything can happen.

Horror has taught me that bad things occur, unexpected things occur, and sometimes the only way out is through. I've somehow stumbled back into my faith, and in that, I have accepted that there is suffering in being human, but that there is also something divine about that suffering. If one has suffered, then one has endured, and if one has endured, one has survived, and here I am, after all this and more. I have endured. My faith is an important part of my life. I don't have a Margaret White–type prayer closet, but prayer and affirmations and gratitude are part of everything I do. And, in terms of my own children, I have learned about the cycles of abuse, from my grandfather to my mother to me, and I stand firm that that cycle of abuse ended with me. When I wake my children in the morning, I tell them I love them, I tell them they're beautiful, I tell them they are great and special, and I shower them with words of praise and blessings throughout the day.

My faith and Stoicism have told me that, yes, bad things happen and, yes, bad people will do bad things, but that no matter what I always have a choice, I always have a choice in how I am going to respond to the awful thing and no monster can take that away from me.

There are nine principles of Stoicism:

1. If you want to live a stress-free life, live so in accordance with the rules of nature.
2. Happiness is not found in things but in virtue.
3. We do not have the power to control external events. We, however, have the power to control our thoughts, opinions, and decisions.
4. We are born with all the inner resources we need to thrive.
5. We have to work as best we can to eliminate toxic emotions like fear.

6. We must remain a unified self, not complaining or blaming anyone else.
7. No one is an island, there are people all around us.
8. Our personal development is connected to others.
9. We must persist and resist: progress is the goal, not perfection.

In looking at these principles, the ones that stand out in my life as being the keys to getting here are accepting that I can always control what I do, what I say, and what I feel; acknowledging that I have always had all the internal resources to navigate my existence; and that regardless, we must persist and resist. And in looking at my love of horror and characters that I have admired in horror films and fiction, I notice too that those characters survived by employing similar methods, utilizing what it was they could control, knowing that the power was always within them, and realizing that in order to survive they had to endure the pain.

This is why I love horror: it validated me, it told me this thing, life, hurts, but you will survive.

Why I Am Horror

By Clay McLeod Chapman

Clay McLeod Chapman plies his trade in discomfort. Yes, his stories are compelling, cinematic, and moving, but they also feature damaged characters whom readers deeply sympathize with, even as they know they probably should not completely trust them. He makes readers squirm with intensely disorienting, anxiety-inducing, visceral, and menacing stories of families in distress, addiction, and, quite often, grief. The palpable terror leaves readers breathless upon initial completion, but then invites them to think about what they just experienced in order to find the hope at the core of it all.

Chapman's essay is framed as a list of his personal "soft traumas" as he articulates how they define his relationship with horror; however, as he goes through, what Chapman calls "soft" gets decidedly more serious, looking at traumas both physical and emotional and digging into how they made him the man he is today. Like Chapman's stories, there is an easy conversational style that allows him to draw the reader in, but also like in his fiction, there are uncomfortable questions, unsettling events, and a serious discussion of how much fear still rules his day-to-day life.

Readers new to Clay McLeod Chapman should start with Ghost Eaters. *For those who want to try a similar author, I suggest Nat Cassidy.*

Why do I love horror? Because it's the f'ing best.

There. Done.

Print that.

An animal's fear impulse protects it from the dangers in the world, triggering its fight-or-flight instinct—so maybe horror is that existential dry run for the myriad predators knocking on mankind's door, rat-a-tat-tapping at our collective defensive measures in order to keep us on our toes. Keep us alive. How many times has horror saved my ass?

Let's see if I can tally them all . . .

"Why can't you just write happy things?" My mother followed this up by saying, "You used to be such a happy boy . . ."

Was I? When did things begin to curdle in her eyes, her son transforming from a cherubic child into this grim scribbler?

When did I find horror? Or maybe more to the point, when did horror find me? Why spend a life being so frightened? Why try to frighten others? Who in the hell does that?

Let's track all the soft traumas. I want to see if I can pinpoint where horror rooted itself into my existence, where my love for the genre began, and try mapping out its course.

Here's my horror autobiography. It is a fool's errand, piecing together an amalgamation of moments from my life in order to better understand the Frankenstein's monster they will eventually make. But I want—need—to know where it all came from.

Maybe this shouldn't be titled "Why I Love Horror" . . . Maybe it's "Why I Need Horror"?

"Why I Have Horror"?

"Why I Am Horror"?

Maybe it was when I fractured my skull.

The first time.

This was when I was two. The way my mother tells the story, I was holstered inside one of those walking strollers. Imagine a plastic doughnut on wheels. Basically, you slip your toddler into this reverse saddle—a cloth diaper, really—wrapped in an elevated plastic ring around their waist and just let 'em go. It helps babies learn how to walk, suspending them on their two feet in an upright, standing position in order to paddle about the house.

Mom was doing the dishes while I was on my little walker walkabout. The door to our basement wasn't fully closed, so when I butted my walker into it, the door simply creaked open and down, down, down I go ... tumbling over twelve wooden steps—*tunk, tunk, tunk*—then *CRACK!*—the back of my skull opened on the concrete floor at the bottom.

Mom heard me shriek. She spotted the basement door wide open and went racing down the steps, finding me on the floor. She scooped me up in her arms—one hand holstering my body, the other supporting my fractured cranium—and rushed out of our house. She ran into the middle of the street, covered in blood, stopping the first car that drove by and begging them to take us to the nearest hospital.

I don't remember any of this, of course, but Mom shared this story with me years later. It's become a well-worn chestnut to tell around the holidays: "Remember that time ..."

Here is my first horror story. The story of my near death. How my life nearly ended before it barely began.

There's a ridge that runs along the back of my head now, just a simple ditch where my skull cracked open. Whenever I'd tell my friends at school this story—my first horror story—I'd even let them run their finger along the slope of my cranium, their pointer skiing down the ragged chasm of bone, as if to prove it all really happened.

Want to feel it? I'll let you the next time we see each other ...

———

Maybe it was the babysitter. John Carpenter's *Halloween* was constantly on television back then, so it was simple to flip the TV on and find this flick on the airwaves. Whether it was a conscious decision on her part or not, my babysitter let me watch . . .

And there he was. Li'l Michael Myers. We were the same age. I kind of even looked like Mike, this despondent child who murdered his own sister/sitter. I watched him on our tiny TV, sitting in a room, staring at a wall, not seeing the wall, looking past the wall, looking at this night, inhumanly patient, waiting for some secret, silent alarm to trigger him . . .

But the freakiest thing about the film was this:

I swore I saw scenes that didn't exist.

I distinctly remember one particular segment where Dr. Loomis slips into young Michael's room at this swanky '70s asylum. Mikey might've tricked the other doctors, but Loomis knows for a fact that there's something evil biding its time inside this boy.

"You've fooled them, haven't you, Michael?" Dr. Loomis says. "But not me . . ."

The next time I watched *Halloween* was on VHS at a friend's house. Someone rented it, and yet, when we sat through it . . . the scene wasn't there, *gone*, like it never even existed. Had I made the moment up? I couldn't have. I remembered it so vividly.

Where did those scenes go? I tried to explain them to my friends, but none of them believed me. We just watched the film. They weren't there. None of them.

I thought I'd lost my mind.

In my head, I believed—truly believed—Carpenter chose me. I had witnessed a version of *Halloween* nobody else had seen. He made it and broadcast it solely for me.

Little did I know that there was a special edit solely for broadcast television that included extra scenes not within the original film. They never tell you this stuff as a kid. They needed to pad their programming to fill a two-hour block, filming extra scenes to kill time.

I thought I was the Chosen One. Michael's disciple.

Maybe it was *Tourist Trap*. Or maybe it was *Saturday the 14th*. Or maybe *Student Bodies*. Back in the early '80s, basic cable channel TBS was able to play toothless—fangless?—horror movies on Saturday afternoons without worry over censors. Nary a parent paid attention to what I viewed, permitting particular flicks to slip under the radar.

Imagine the pre-PG-13 era. My early childhood dovetailed perfectly with Steven Spielberg's early '80s Amblin output, exposing my preadolescent film-viewing mind to the likes of *Gremlins* and *Poltergeist* and heart-ripping Kali Ma before the MPA caught on.

I was a latchkey kid. Nobody was watching me, so I was watching it all...

Maybe it was the *Challenger*. Our entire fourth grade class hunkered down on the carpet as Mrs. Green wheeled out a boxy television set on a rolling cart. We tuned in to view the live broadcast of this historic occasion, much like so many other kids across the country.

We all watched the shuttle disintegrate on live TV. We couldn't look away. Not until Mrs. Green turned off the television. The screen slipped into blackness as she struggled to articulate what we had all just witnessed. There were no words, only tears. I found myself wanting Mrs. Green to turn the TV back on, to rewind, do a do-over, take it all back, but it was too late by then. The sky went wild with fire, orange blossoms enveloping the shuttle, burning into my brain so that it played and replayed over and over again in my imagination.

Maybe it was Hank. There was a stepfather in my life for about three years. Between the ages of six and nine, my mother was married to a man who was subtly abusive in ways that, even to this day, I'm still trying to understand. I constantly accost my own memory of this man because I don't know if I can trust my recollections of him. There is a black hole at the center of my childhood and it's swallowed up three years of my life.

I was a kid. Just a scared kid.

My perspective may have been skewed by childhood, but this was when I learned to be frightened of people. That human beings are capable of harm. Adults can do bad things.

I remember night terrors. Debilitating dreams. Wetting my bed. I remember peeing in a cup because I couldn't bring myself to wander down the hall to our bathroom. The shadows in my bedroom were alive, pools of oily ink that moved with intent, seeping into my sheets and swallowing me whole. I started falling asleep in class at school, unable to stay awake. My teachers expressed a concern that I wasn't getting enough rest at home.

I have memories of visiting a therapist of some sort, a special doctor whose office was made of burnished wood. I remember deep, dark varnish. This doctor wanted to talk to me about my experiences. I was shown puppets—dolls—and asked if they might help tell my story. Was I supposed to point to particular spots on them? *What am I supposed to do?*

Whenever I bring these memories up with my mother . . . she tells me they never happened. Hank was real, yes. But the night terrors? The therapy? Nothing, nothing at all.

Our versions of Hank vary to an unnerving degree. Did I make it up? Why?

Hank was a member of our household. He was the fundamental presence in my mind for years, but now . . . he's fading from our family's narrative, like he never existed.

Poof.

I don't know what I'm supposed to believe or what I can consider real or imaginary. There's something so isolating about not being able to connect with my mother over these memories, to feel this siloed from one of the most pivotal periods of my childhood.

Why can't you just write happy things? You used to be such a happy boy . . .

Maybe it was the drowned cow. There's a particular patch of road that runs alongside the James River, perfect for riding bikes. There had been a flood recently, so there was far more flotsam along the shore to explore, all the washed-up junk to sift through.

I remember climbing across a few fallen branches, stepping over a tangle of limbs, before stumbling upon the bloated body of a cow. The flood must've whisked it off from whatever farm it lived on and sent it farther downriver, its body washing up miles away. Its belly was so distended, it looked like a massive water balloon about to burst. I swear it didn't have any fur on it, pale and pink and smooth skin. Here was death, washed up to me.

Maybe it was when I fractured my skull for the second time.

This time I was five. Five or six.

Mom took me to the county fair. I broke away from her and raced through the crowd, bobbing and weaving around all the older, taller adults, simply giddy to be in the mix of games and rides. I must not have been paying attention to where I was going, getting clotheslined by a couple holding hands as they headed in the opposite direction. I ran right into them, their arms hooking me in the jaw and flipping me over. I fell backward like a clumsy acrobat and landed right on the tip of a tent spike, cracking my head open yet again.

True story. How am I still alive?

Maybe it was *The Stuff*. Just the trailer. It was my best friend Billy Droste's birthday party and we were at the movies. He picked *Godzilla 1985*, which I don't remember much of, but I definitely remember the trailers. This particular preview was fashioned into a PSA, warning audience members to steer clear of a particular frozen confection invading the dairy aisles of our supermarkets . . . the Stuff. It looked like ice cream. Tasted like ice cream. But it was actually some sort of sentient gloop that emerged from the earth to devour hapless customers, a coy commentary on consumerism by none other than Larry Cohen, perfectly summed up by the film's tagline: "Are you eating it . . . or is it eating you?"

I didn't have the maturity to understand that this was all pretend. The preview had the verisimilitude of an actual PSA, at least to me, so I genuinely believed there was a brand of monstrous ice cream on the shelves now, consuming consumers from the inside out.

Now I had to be cautious about my ice cream. Was nothing sacred in this world? Just how many monsters were out there, trying to eat me?

Maybe it was *Scary Stories to Tell in the Dark* by Alvin Schwartz. The stories, yes, but . . . my God, those illustrations by Stephen Gammell never left my subconscious.

I still have "The Hearse Song" rattling about my head. I can recite it from memory.

But maybe, more likely, it was *Monsters of North America* by William Wise. A slight precursor to *Scary Stories*, *Monsters of North America* focused on the myths and urban legends that seeped out from the folklore of the region around us. It felt so close. *Closer.*

As a kid, my grandmother made a deal with me. Whenever I stayed at my grandparents' place, which was often back then, she'd take me to the local library and I'd be allowed to check out two books—any two—one of which she'd read to me, the other I'd read to myself. For me, I always picked something like *The Far Side*, while for her, I'd pick something heftier.

That's where the Wendigo first entered my life.

To this day, I can remember my grandmother reading from *Monsters of North America*, recounting the tale of two hapless fur trappers encountering a malevolent presence in the wintry woods, whisking one away so fast and forcing him to run, run, run, his feet were reduced to nothing more than ash. There's a charcoal drawing in the book, a full two-page spread with no text, showing a man running through the sky, his eyes and mouth smeared shadows. That single image meant so much to me. Years later, I hunted the book, long out of print, down on eBay and bought it, just to see those eyes again.

To be haunted all over again.

Maybe it was Matt and Jamie Walker. Jamie was my age. Matt was his older brother. They lorded over our neighborhood with a cool brutality that bruised the rest of us kids.

Matt scored a VHS copy of Wes Craven's *Deadly Friend*. Their parents ordered pizza. There had to be five or six of us, all crowded on the couch in their basement, watching this odd flick about a teen genius who transfers a microchip into the body of his dead neighbor.

When we reached the scene where a robotic Kristy Swanson picks up a basketball and rockets it directly at Anne Ramsey's head, shattering her skull with the ease of smashing a melon, I turned away out of revulsion. I had to be, what, eight? Nine?

Matt clocked my disgust and turned it into a teaching moment. He grabbed me from behind, bear-hugging me so I couldn't escape. He ordered his baby brother to rewind the scene on the VHS player so I had to watch it again. And again. Who knows how many times this went on, but Matt forced me to watch Anne Ramsey's cranium explode repeatedly— a soupy loop of practical effects in slow motion—while the rest of the kids from the neighborhood laughed at my queasy expense. If I turned away, if I closed my eyes, Matt would add another rewind to my sentence. I was physically restrained, forced against my will to watch this act of absurd violence like this was all some suburban version of *A Clockwork Orange*. It wasn't until I relented, leaning into the carnage and taking it all in, that Matt Walker grew bored with his torture and I was finally, mercifully released.

But by then, the damage was done.

I hated basketball.

Maybe it was Tailypo. In the summer between fifth and sixth grade, I went to my first overnight camp at Holiday Lake 4-H Camp in Appomattox, Virginia.

It was here, around the campfire, that I experienced my first ghost story. One of our counselors regaled us with the tale of a miserly hunter and his two dogs coming upon a creature that defied God's provenance—shooting it, severing its tail, and cooking it in a stew—only for that creature to come crawling back for its tailypo later that night.

Here was storytelling distilled: I vividly remember the campfire. The flames licking at my counselor's face. Campers' cheeks bathed in orange. But there was a whole story happening at my back as well—a story untold, no words, full of sounds and senses, written within the woods, in the dark, where the light of our fire couldn't reach, waiting for me.

Suddenly I was aware of the story expanding in my imagination, embracing the surrounding trees and everything within them, the things I couldn't see.

I took the story into my body and continued to tell it even after the night was done.

That's the night I discovered a story needs to seep into your senses. It must take over every sensory organ—sight, sound, touch, smell, taste— consuming you just as much as you consume it. *Are you the one listening to a ghost story . . . or is the ghost story listening to you?*

Maybe it was Video World. The lighting in the horror section always seemed to be a bit darker, the carpet a bit dingier, than the rest of the video store. Something about that particular aisle felt far more dangerous. The shelves were filled with VHS cassette covers that displayed singular images of violence and depravity that seared their way into my eleven-year-old subconscious. Each sleeve had its own horror story to tell. They were artwork in their own right, and I felt like I was wandering through a museum, marveling at this monstrosity exhibit suspended on the walls. *Evil Dead II. Troll. Prince of Darkness.* I may have been far too young to rent the movies themselves, but I didn't need to for these films to have an impact on me. The stories I made up in my imagination, simply by poring over their cassette sleeves, was enough to fill my head with nightmares to last me for years. The movies I made up tended to be even scarier than the actual films.

Maybe it was Edgar Allan Poe. His first-person narratives taught me all about direct address, bringing in the reader as if they are somehow complicit in the story being told. Reading his stories, I felt like I was a part of the action. Trapped somehow. An audience of one, dragged in by his narrators. Now I couldn't escape. Nothing in me wanted to. I was sitting at the campfire all over again, being regaled by a tale that needed me in order to exist. These stories were alive. They possessed breath. They were all mine.

Maybe it was Stephen King. It's inevitable. All roads lead back to the King. I remember sitting in my seventh-grade English class, not paying attention to whatever my teacher was talking about, focusing all my energy on the paperback of *Night Shift* in my lap, hidden underneath my desk. I got caught, of course, my copy confiscated ... which is when I picked up *Skeleton Crew*. No lie, those two collections are without a doubt the most formative fodder for my love of horror and the beginning of my education in how to tell scary stories.

Maybe it was "The Snowman."

I wrote a short story for school about a snowman who comes to life and kills the kids who made it. Maybe not a masterpiece ... but the note from my teacher to my mother really sealed the deal: "The morose subject matter of Clay's fiction is of concern at school," he wrote, "but I won't make assumptions about his emotional and psychological well-being."

I was thirteen. When I read those words, how unnerved this teacher was over something I had written, I couldn't help but think, *I can make people feel this way?*

I kept the letter. Still have it.

Maybe it was *Spoon River Anthology* by Edgar Lee Masters.

Maybe it was the poetry of Ai.

Maybe it's Josh Malerman. Ronald Malfi. Rachel Harrison. Daniel Kraus. Stephen Graham Jones. CJ Leede. Eric LaRocca. Nat Cassidy. Tananarive Due. Cassandra Khaw. Chuck Wendig. Alison Rumfitt. Paul Tremblay. Gabino Iglesias. Alma Katsu. Adam Nevill. Catriona Ward.

Maybe it's David Cronenberg. John Carpenter. Wes Craven. Tobe Hooper. Sam Raimi. Bob Clark.

Maybe it's Ari Aster. Jennifer Kent. Mike Flanagan. Robert Eggers. Jordan Peele. Karyn Kusama.

Maybe it's my kids. One of the most frightening things in my life, as a parent, is that I have to let go of my children on a daily basis. Just let them loose into this world. I kiss them goodbye and the world is theirs to navigate, while I sit here in my office and imagine the absolute worst possible occurrences that may befall them. It's not uncommon to ask myself: *Please, no school shootings today. Please, no tragedies. Let them come home safe.*

I am afraid for them. So unbelievably afraid.

I cast my kids in my own private horror movies, day after day. The way I offer myself catharsis, struggling to exorcize all these pent-up fears, is to write them out of my system.

They're your nightmares now.

———

The night before I started writing this piece, I had a dream. Maybe it was a nightmare? Another student's parent from my eldest son's school complained to the admin about my writing, outing me as a horror author. She was concerned my books weren't appropriate for younger readers and I shouldn't be allowed anywhere near the students. This is what was occupying my mind just a few hours ago before diving into this . . .

The fear doesn't end. It never goes away. It simply evolves. Mutates. Permutates.

What horrors do I have to face today?

What am I afraid of *now*?

Do you see why I need horror? Is there something lingering within the stitchwork of this Frankenstein's monster of my life that amounts to that spark—the soul—of fear? Love?

I love horror. I am horror.

What does it add up to? A frightened child. A frightened adult.

A life spent being afraid of everything.

A life in horror.

Maybe you should write your own horror autobiography. Now it's your turn. See if you can pinpoint the moment(s) where horror roots itself into your life. Where fear takes over. How you process it. Internalize—then externalize—those nightmares. To share your story.

Tell us . . . why do you love horror?

We're listening.

A Day in My Psychedelic World

By Nuzo Onoh

Nuzo Onoh has been referred to as the Queen of African Horror. The British Nigerian author and scholar is the mother of a generation of new African horror voices making a name for themselves writing in English. Evil is in a constant battle against the forces of good in Onoh's works. African folklore, evocative prose, and, always, a spiritual tone work in tandem to draw readers from across the globe into her immersive tales. While Onoh's stories are clearly centered on the supernatural, readers will find a truth at the core of these dark fantasy tales and will not be able to help seeing themselves in her characters.

Onoh's essay is written in a similar style to her novels: it is a fever dream as she conjures up evocative images and injects all five senses into the words on the page. But it is also an honest story of trauma, of chronic insomnia, of intense fear since the COVID-19 lockdowns, and of a woman for whom the comfort she finds in horror has had to change as a result.

Readers new to Nuzo Onoh should start with Where the Dead Brides Gather. *For those who want to try a similar author, I suggest Tobi Ogundiran.*

⎯⎯⎯⎯

I t's 3:00 a.m. in the wee hours of the night. The rain lashes gently on my windowpane, and as always, sleep and I continue our failing marriage, even as we share my body and bed in what has become a restless union. Briefly, I consider drawing my blinds to see the crystal raindrops trailing the glass sheets of my window; but I quickly quash that thought—*Uh-uh, can't take the risk of exposing myself to any vampires lurking outside my window.* I don't question the rationality of this thought, just as I never doubt the possibility of flying vampires each time I use the subway pedestrian passage into town. At least there are CCTV cameras in the subway to record my demise. I have no such protection inside my bedroom, though. My blinds remain shut, just like my bolted bedroom door—after all, no one will save me if evil aliens invade my home, and at sixty years plus, I doubt my ability to overcome any little green men that might break through my unlocked door . . . (By the way, thank you, Brian Duffield, for ruining my peace. Watch the film *No One Will Save You* to appreciate my seemingly irrational fears.)

But hearken! Against all odds, all is well in my twilight world. Despite my thoughts of evil vampires and invading aliens, I feel cosy instead of terrified. My soul vibrates with warm serenity and joy. Every pore in my body tingles with that special excitement that tells us everything is just fine and a special treat awaits us. My duvet is softly welcoming and the lyrics of the song playing quietly on my bedstand speakers fill me with bliss.

I can't resist another delicious sigh. "Spanish Train" by Chris de Burgh always delivers. Nothing beats listening quietly to music while cosied up in bed on a rainy night, with or without a lover. Soon, "Spanish Train" is followed by "Hotel California," then "Bohemian Rhapsody" and "Goodnight Saigon," on and on and on, as my horror-themed playlist continues to heal any emotional traumas that might usually accompany my congenital insomnia. Harrowing memories of past experiences that would normally rear up their vile faces are annihilated by the haunting, poetic, and savage lyrics of these classics, and once again, I whisper a soft and fervent thank-you to the universe for the gift of horror in all its glorious forms: music, films, theatre, literature, arts.

Somehow, I make it through the long night to the dull winter's morn, and soon, I'm settled in my seat on the train to London. I have an important meeting that will take me away from my small city, and I can't wait to savour another opportunity to ride the train. It's not a particularly busy coach, and I observe a few of my fellow passengers with lazy interest—*Hmm . . . I wonder if that guy in the snazzy blue suit has just murdered his pregnant mistress and is now returning to his unsuspecting pregnant wife. Yeah . . . something about his weak jawline and shifty eyes tells me he's dodgy . . . And oh dear Lord! Look at that thing sitting at the bottom table wearing those weird sunglasses in the middle of winter. I bet it's an alien who doesn't want us to see its strange-coloured eyes. I'm sure that long woollen hat hides its spiked ears.* Suddenly, I'm thinking that I should google to see if there were any unusual sightings or unexplained activities last night during the storm. One never knows when we could be called upon as witnesses if it turns out we shared a train with an alien from Mars.

The train pulls away from the station. I shrug and pull out my latest read, *The Fifth Child* by Doris Lessing. It's a small book that fits snugly inside my handbag and makes for an easy, leisurely read filled with tension and that special kind of buzz that only true horror can induce. This is the kind of horror I enjoy, psychological horror, amongst other subcategories of the genre. That's another great thing about horror: there's always something for every taste and everyone—ghost and supernatural horror, slasher/gore horror, monsters and creatures horror, sci-fi and alien horror, cosmic horror, gothic horror, folk horror, dystopian horror, apocalyptic ancient disease horror, witches, vampires, werewolves, zombies, mythological creatures, everything in between. You name it, there's something there in the genre pool for every horror buff, and I'm holding my own treat right now.

Soon, I'm lost in a new world, my fellow murderous and alien passengers clean forgotten as the train eats up the miles on its metal path. I even forget to indulge in another one of my travel pastimes and fail to reenact my favourite *The Girl on the Train* role. I see no tragic cheating heroines or dodgy randy shrinks or murderous exes lurking in scenic English houses and villages. Instead, the usual quaint and likely haunted church graveyards and old, abandoned, and, again, likely haunted brick houses disappear from my view as I marinate in the creepy feast of my latest horror treat until the announcer's robotic voice jolts me out of the magic. I've arrived at my final destination. *London! That was fast! What a beautiful journey I've had, thanks to my horror novel.*

I put away my book and mobile phone as I grab my winter coat from the empty seat next to mine. I'm still buzzing from the gripping story I read during the journey, and even the murderer turns out to be a lovely chap after all, as he smiles nicely at me and lets me go through the exit first. *Perfect gentleman, definitely not a cheating murderous love rat.* As for the alien in the dark sunglasses, just another unconventional Gen Z with attitude and swagger—*Just see how he's strutting off nodding his head to the music from those massive headphones he now dons. Bet it's killing his eardrums.*

I shake my head wryly with a little smile as I exit Euston station. I can hardly wait for the return journey so I can enmesh myself in the book again and see what that weird child, Ben, has been up to in the story. Once again, I give a silent thanks for the gift of horror that just keeps giving and giving. One never ceases to be surprised and amazed at the unfathomable depths the human mind can descend into when crafting horror. There's always something new to inspire you, astonish you, confound you; some incredible feat of imagination displayed by yet another writer, director, artist, or creative to terrify and entertain. I'm always in awe of the writing prowess of countless peers and so grateful for the opportunity to discover exciting new voices in the ever-expanding speculative talent pool.

With horror as my companion, there's no time for boredom or restlessness. It keeps my imagination active, wild, and mega-creative. Even as I relax inside the return train home after my London jaunt, I manage to catch a glimpse of a windmill through the dusty windows of the train. By the time I get home, I've already typed a brief summary of a short story on my mobile, where the windmill blades detach in a ghastly accident and decapitate a poor maiden hanging her laundry. Her legs and hips go one direction while her head and upper torso flee in another direction, carried away by the hurricane winds that caused the windmill malfunction. Now each body part is desperately seeking reunification with the other while petrifying dog-walking pensioners into heart attacks and early graves. Between this little story and Doris Lessing's horror book, my journey home is a roaring success and an ode to the power of horror to keep the mind, heart, and body excitedly engaged, alive, joyful, and fulfilled.

Back home, I shower off the grime of the London Underground experience, change into my tatty and comfy home wear, order a Chinese takeaway, and settle down before the telly to de-stress. It's still taking me a while to accept that my feline companion, Tinkerbell, is gone and we now share the house by ourselves: me, myself, and I.

My chair faces my favourite bookshelf that houses my favourite reads. I enjoy looking at the books and reminiscing over the ones I've read while debating the next ones to explore in my TBR. Old favourites meet my avid gaze: Stephen King in different sizes and covers, Yōko Ogawa, Amos Tutuola, Ira Levin, Anne Rice, etc., etc., etc. Some new ones also hold place of honour on my special small shelf: *The Ghost Bride* by Yangsze Choo, *Among the Living* by Tim Lebbon, *Mage of Fools* by Eugen Bacon, *The Pallbearers Club* by Paul Tremblay, *Summer, Fireworks, and My Corpse* by Otsuichi, *The Path of Thorns* by A. G. Slatter, amongst several others I can't mention for lack of space.

Soon, the Uber delivery guy knocks on my front door—*my supper has arrived, yippee!* I settle into my favourite comfy chair and turn on the TV to find Nicolas Cage is rocking it in *Pay the Ghost*, and my world is all right once again despite the slight unease I feel. But it's a film I've watched several times, and Nic Cage is an actor I've fancied in the past amongst so many other male hunks, so I'm not too terrified to watch this film alone. Did I just say terrified? Yes, I did, and you'll soon find out why.

By the time the film ends, I am complete; my soul is satisfied and my body saturated with the pork fried rice and fortune cookies I always get for my dessert. I ordered four fortune cookies tonight and all my predictions are very positive ones. And when I WhatsApp my daughters at the end of the day to let them know their mama hasn't been abducted by aliens or turned by a vampire's bite or possessed by malevolent entities while alone in her empty house, I can hear their relief and joy. Their mother might be living alone, but she's never lonely. They know me and my vivid, psychedelic imagination too well. As long as there's creative horror in music, books, films, and theatres, I can look defiantly into the world and its miseries and bellow in my fakest American accent, "Bring it on, you MFs!"

And at the end of an eventful and fulfilling day, as I stretch out on my bed once again, eager to read the last chapter of *The Fifth Child* before calling it a day, I hear the dulcet voice of one of my favourite actors, Charles Dance, whisper in my head, "Let the games begin." *Damn! I really must watch* Dracula Untold *again soon. Who cares if I've watched it five times already? Luke Evans never fails to deliver.*

I fall asleep eventually at some point during the night, and as expected, the dreams, the nightmares, arrive in force. As always, I'm fighting ghosts in gloomy, strange worlds and familiar spaces, flying over trees and houses to escape faceless demons, bargaining with witches and aliens while killing snakes and roaches. And when I finally wake up, I know I have another inspiration for a future story as I quickly scribble my nightmares into my dream diary. *Job well done, Nuzo!*

And so another day in my mundane life passes with no mega events to ruin my romance with horror, save the wacky thoughts and imaginings killing my common sense, together with the nightmares ruining my sleep. I reckon everyone reading this now knows why I absolutely love horror. To me, horror is soul food, a balm for troubled minds. Writing horror has been an exorcism for me in many ways, as I consciously and subconsciously channel past harrowing experiences and dump them within the pages of my fiction stories. Beats a shrink any day.

Best of all, horror affords me and other creatives the freedom to critique anything that bothers us without fear of recriminations. We've seen the powerful political impact of the books *Nineteen Eighty-Four* and *Animal Farm*. Films like Jordan Peele's *Get Out* and *Us* are like society's mirrors, reflecting back to us the ills and moral bankruptcies of the world we live in. Through the fictitious means of horror, these works and others like them explore and expose controversial and explosive topics and issues without incurring the negative ramifications that might follow a nonfiction work. So, we can say that horror gives us a safe space to vent on issues that bother us, just as I've used it in my books to vent on such issues as ritual murders, caste systems, brutal widowhood rites, patriarchy and misogyny, child abuse, and the scourge of unscrupulous witch doctors and religious quacks in African societies.

For me, horror is also an escape from tormented reality, a sanctuary from the brutalities of the true horror known as humanity. Within its fantastical cocoon, I'm safe in the knowledge that such evils can never happen to me, only to others in some unknown place and realm. I can escape from the nightmare realities of the world and its miseries, lost in horror's magic for that brief spell. During the Biafran War, as I grew up surrounded by daily deaths from both the Nigerian bombs and deadly kwashiorkor sickness, the nightly "Tales by Moonlight" sessions brought wonderful respite to me. Those tales featured predominantly terrifying ghosts and demon entities, mighty deities, powerful witch doctors, evil witches, wicked stepmothers, stupendous transmogrifications, and clever, cunning animals, as well as a great deal of fantastical magic. I could forget the day terrors of the war during those "Tales by Moonlight" sessions, and that wonderful sense of security in horror followed me into my adulthood, eventually influencing my writing. I guess that's why I always experience this instinctive delicious feeling of cosiness whenever I come across a horror book or film, before any cowardly thoughts can intrude to mar things for me. I think that's also why the pandemic hit me very hard, because, suddenly, Stephen King had entered my world in the worst possible way. *The Stand* was supposed to remain in the realm of the cosy fantastical, but now, it had breached the fortress and entered our lives with horrible reality. I felt very betrayed and never read or watched a single work of horror for the two-year duration of the lockdown.

But all that apart, horror allows me to explore myself on a deeper level outside my normal self-awareness. It is a soul mirror that forces me to confront my moral compass, my resilience, my core values and beliefs: Can I really swear that I *definitely will not* eat my fellow passengers if we're stranded on a deserted island for months after a plane crash? What will I do if aliens really do arrive, or a zombie apocalypse occurs, ancestors forbid such evil? Will I sacrifice my fellow humans to save myself or be heroic like Seok-woo in *Train to Busan*? Will I sell my soul to the aliens (the 1984 TV series *V*) or fearlessly take on the battle like Michonne (*The Walking Dead*)? Am I really sure I can take up that writing residency in the cosy eighteenth-century cottage nestled within the old churchyard overlooking the ancient graveyard? *Really, Nuzo? Even with your terror of ghosts and vivid imagination and unreasonable superstitions? Actually, maybe not . . . not even for all the benefits of the grant and residency. I should know my limitations and avoid sacrificing my mental well-being for greed. We definitely won't be applying for this particular residency, thank you very much.*

This is who I am, an unapologetic wuss who surrounds herself with numerous crystals to ward off the evil eye and negativity and must always sleep with the lights on. Nonetheless, I'm glad for this self-reflection and insight obtained via the medium of horror. I think I know myself a bit better thanks to all the horror books and films I've enjoyed. So, yeah, as the great Bard would say, "To thine own self be true," Nuzo Onoh. I now accept that I am a horror writer who has become terrified of horror even as I continue to write it and automatically gravitate to it. As the great Al Jarreau sang, "We're in this love together."

Okay, I think I've gone a bit deeper than I planned when sharing my love of horror. So, I'll just complete this tête-à-tête by sharing a little secret about horror and me. Remember I mentioned a slight unease and something about not being too terrified to watch Nic Cage in the film *Pay the Ghost*? Well, come closer and I'll elucidate.

Yes, I write horror. I've even been dubbed the Queen of African Horror by fans and the media. As you've seen so far, my mind is so messed up that I can't ever see anything or rationalise the most benign stuff without going down the proverbial rabbit hole of horror. Even when we had a slight earth tremor that shook the house enough to cause my table to slide, I immediately ran out of the room screaming, "Ghosts!" By the time my neighbours joined me outside that unforgettable night, I had changed my mind to aliens, positive that a mother ship had landed nearby. At one point, I even crept back into my house, convinced that all my neighbours gathered outside in the street were at risk of being zapped by the aliens just as they did in *Independence Day*.

So, what am I saying? Basically, I always seek and believe a supernatural cause or hand in every innocuous occurrence. Blown bulb? Poltergeist! Sudden cat mewing? An invisible presence in the room! Sleep paralysis? Demon entities have come for me! Hell, I even abandoned a good career as a licenced funeral celebrant because I was convinced I'd brought home the ghost of one of my clients. I ended up chucking away the clothes I wore for that particular funeral, and now, I no longer send the dead away with beautifully scripted and delivered eulogies. I've only written my own eulogy for my kids to read when I'm gone.

So, with all these, it won't come as a surprise to learn that I'm terrified of horror even as I'm irresistibly drawn to it. As a fiction writer, I can only write horror. Even when I attempt humour, horror inevitably creeps into the narrative. I'm still the first to visit graveyards and cemeteries to read the writings on gravestones and always excited to read about near-death experiences. I still pester people to tell me their ghost stories and experiences of the paranormal.

Yet, these days, especially since the COVID-19 lockdown, I struggle to watch horror films by myself. Because of my insomnia, when I'm lucky to sleep, I dream extremely vivid and psychedelic dreams, as I mentioned. But I find that my mind is so screwed up that I now dream of whatever I watch on the telly or at the cinema, but thankfully, not what I read. So, since I live alone and am not yet blessed with a third and final husband to protect me from the malevolent unknown, horror films and I have now mostly parted ways, alas. But that day, I gave Nic Cage a chance and I made it through, but don't expect us to be chilling in the cinema watching a horror movie should we ever meet and hang out in the flesh.

I still read horror books, albeit not as voraciously as in the past and never in the night as before. These days, I read my horror mostly among the living, and it still brings me something I need, a need I have tried to explain through my psychedelic, wacky world of superstitious horror. And it's not just me. Let us celebrate the beautiful cultural holidays and festivals that remember their dead: the Nigerian Odo festival, UK/USA Halloween, Mexican Día de los Muertos, Madagascan Famadihana ("turning of the bones"), the Japanese Obon festival, the Korean Chuseok festival, the Chinese Hungry Ghost and Qingming festivals, Hindu Pitru Paksha, and more. Long may we live before crossing behind that thin veil of mystery and eternity.

Permission to Scream

By Rachel Harrison

Rachel Harrison is the voice of millennial horror, exploring relationships of all types between friends, family members, lovers. She has a string of critically acclaimed novels that explore the horrors of being a woman at this moment in history. In menacing, creepy, and even at times gruesome detail, Harrison leaves nothing out, something readers of all genders appreciate. Her stories ring true because they are honest, but she also pairs that honesty with a conversational style and biting dark humor, drawing readers into her worlds immediately; however, it is her thought-provoking social commentary that brings them all back for more.

Harrison's essay marks an entry point for the next three authors, who write at length about their coming of age both as humans and as horror writers. These authors not only found their voice in print, but they also found agency in their lives by embracing horror. For Harrison, horror became the place where she could take her revenge on the horrors society inflicts upon young women. She writes about dress codes, the beauty paradox, and light yogurt. This essay is very much in the style of her fiction writing, and it adds a lot of insight into not only where her ideas come from, but also why her novels have become so popular—they hit very close to home.

Readers new to Rachel Harrison should start with Such Sharp Teeth. *For those who want to try a similar author, I suggest Lindy Ryan.*

———

Sometimes I think about this yogurt commercial. Sorry, this *light* yogurt commercial. A woman in a loose sweatshirt walks past a bikini hanging on her wall while she eats this yogurt, as "Itsy Bitsy Teenie Weenie Yellow Polka Dot Bikini" by Brian Hyland plays in the background. She continues to walk past the bikini on the wall while eating yogurt, now wearing a robe, now in business casual, now in an evening dress, until finally, she puts the bikini on—albeit under shorts and a tank top. She hops in a car, presumably on her way to the beach. A confident voice-over boasts that it's "clinically shown" this yogurt will help you burn more fat than just cutting calories alone! Imagine! Wow. Amazing.

I was subjected to this commercial as a teenager, along with millions of other impressionable young Americans, which is reason enough to grow into adulthood with a feral rage simmering under the surface. But the thing is, I ate this fucking yogurt. My mom bought this fucking yogurt.

How much bland, watery light yogurt did I shovel into my mouth thinking that's what I needed to do to feel good about myself, to be accepted by society? How much time and energy did I dedicate to making myself smaller? To taking up less space? Too much. And I can never get it back. It breaks my heart and makes me so angry I could scream. But since I can't John Wick whatever marketing executives signed off on that bullshit or take down diet culture single-handedly, my only path to vengeance is on the page.

This is why I love horror. It's my retribution.

But I don't want to give yogurt too much credit; it turns out I'm lactose intolerant. It's not just about the commercial or that flavored milk water I thought I needed to guzzle for clearance to wear a bikini.

Cut to Mount Olive Middle School. It's 2003. Aragorn is king, Beyoncé's gone solo, and, in general, things are pretty good. Except that I'm in eighth grade and in this assembly called by our vice principal, who bears a startling resemblance to Miss Trunchbull. This assembly is about the dress code. It's just for girls.

"*T. M. I.* Too. Much. Information!" VP Trunchbull yells. No spaghetti straps. Skirts must be at least fingertip length. Nothing low-cut because it's distracting to our classmates, aka the boys, who got to stay in class and presumably learn while we were being lectured.

A few weeks later, I was heading into fifth period. My teacher stopped me. "Don't you think that skirt is a little short?" she asked.

It was a jean skirt well past fingertip length, and I was a painfully shy rule-following thirteen-year-old with braces and a bad haircut. I wasn't dressing provocatively, trying to get the attention of my classmates—I wasn't interested in the boys at my school, I had a crush on Orlando Bloom as both Legolas *and* Will Turner—and this teacher knew it. It was sweltering outside, and our school was stuffy and hot. Should I have worn snow pants?

I apologized to my teacher and promised I wouldn't wear it again. I remember the shame I felt walking to my desk, tears stinging my eyes. There was so much external pressure to look a certain way that I'd been tortured by since childhood, that led me to a debilitating eating disorder, but now entering adolescence, I was being told that looking this certain way was bad.

My body needed to look just so to be acceptable, but I also needed to cover it. If I showed my body, I was a slut. I was asking for it. But I still needed to be pretty. Just not the kind of pretty that would invite trouble.

I wish someone had told me then that it doesn't matter what you look like. What you wear. What you do or don't do. What you eat, or if you starve. The cruelties of this world are not discerning.

I don't know what it's like to feel safe inside my skin. I am hyperaware of my appearance at all times. I am constantly at odds with my body, the vessel I live inside. My house is haunted. It's cursed. It's been invaded. It's betrayed me. I hate it. I love it. I need it. I can't ever leave.

This is why I love horror. It understands.

There's an interesting phenomenon I've noticed with women, perhaps especially millennial women, where we're in this perpetual state of war with "supposed to." For some, it's a cold war, a historical war. For others it's a full-on battle. We're stuck fighting between societal expectations and our own aspirations. How do we even tell the difference? Do we want to be wives and mothers and homemakers, or is that what society expects of us? Do we want to pursue our careers and become wildly successful, or is that ambition somehow manufactured to rebel against the patriarchy? We have more choices than ever before, but somehow every open door feels like a trapdoor.

We're supposed to be youthful and beautiful, but our beauty makes us prey. We're supposed to age gracefully, but also inject chemicals into our faces so we're still nice to look at, because if we aren't nice to look at, we lose our value. We're not supposed to be jealous or petty or mean, we're supposed to support other women, but not be *so* positive that it's toxic. We're supposed to love ourselves, but we must hate ourselves or else entire industries would collapse.

And as we try to figure out what to do and how to be, our choices are being stripped away from us. Crusty old men and religious zealots sit on the Supreme Court controlling our bodily autonomy. Dumbass football players give commencement speeches riddled with hate and a message that women's place is in the home—a message on the rise, this return to "tradition." Trad wives, all that.

Why do I love horror? It's catharsis. It's where my characters rage against this ceaseless, dizzying, infuriating bullshit.

It took a while, though, for me to recognize my love of the genre. I was not a child with a particular interest in the macabre. I was a smidge morbid, a bit death-obsessed, thanks to a fascination with fairy tales, but I was also an easily frightened, slightly (okay, incredibly) dramatic, sensitive, sugary princess. I loved movies as a kid, and my mother was happy to encourage my cinematic curiosities. I'd seen *Jaws* and *Alien* before I learned how to add and subtract, and to this day, I can't dip a toe into a body of water or look up at the night sky without immense anxiety. I loved stories, but there was never any buffer between me and the stories I consumed. My suspension of disbelief is faulty—my pause button, broken. Once I believe, once I let a story in, it takes up permanent residence.

One of my earliest memories is of going on the Haunted Mansion ride at Disney World. I was five or six years old, we were waiting in line, and I was getting wary the closer we got to the attraction. There was the distant sound of werewolf howls, the mansion looming large, the chill of standing in its massive shadow. I relayed my growing concern to my mother, who assured me the ride was more "funny than scary."

Well, not for baby me! The ride kicks off with finding out your ghostly narrator hanged himself in the mansion, and his ghastly figure is projected above you, swinging from a noose. Super child-friendly, right? I had nightmares for weeks. I was consumed with thoughts of the hanging man. I would sleep with the covers over my head, leaving only a tiny hole for my nose and mouth so I could breathe. I was terrified that if I were to look up at the ceiling, he'd be hanging there. I insisted upon an additional night-light—effective ghost deterrents, of course.

Because of this, I thought I didn't like horror. I would get scared if I merely glanced at a horror movie cover at Blockbuster (RIP) or saw a creepy book at the library (the irony). Spooky stories from classmates or cousins would completely take over my life. If it isn't already painfully apparent by this point in the essay, I'm an anxious person with an inherent flair for dramatics and a negative attitude. Why invite more anxiety into my life? More fear? More opportunities to obsess over everything that could possibly go horribly wrong. I had enough issues. Why pile on?

I did still dabble here and there. I'd watch a slasher with a crush so we could hide under the same blanket, read Stephen King or Shirley Jackson, sit through one of the scarier episodes of *The Twilight Zone* during the marathons on New Year's Eve or over the Fourth of July. But it wasn't until college that I had my epiphany.

My friend and suite mate Maria was a certified horror junkie. Freshman year, she gathered the roommates on a snowy weekend for back-to-back viewings of *The Shining*—Stanley Kubrick's version and the TV miniseries. On a rainy day sophomore year, the two of us were hanging out twisting open Oreos and licking out the cream, and she put on J. A. Bayona's *The Orphanage*. I made it about halfway through, then had a massive panic attack and had to stop watching. I went back to my room and hyperventilated, my heartbeat erratic (in retrospect that could have been because of all the Oreos—I don't know, I'm not a doctor). I can't remember what finally calmed me down; all I remember is marching back to Maria's room the next day and asking if we could finish the movie. I could not stop thinking about it. Despite my fear, despite how much the film made me feel, or maybe *because* of how much it made me feel, I needed to know what happened. I was so compelled. The story was already in me. I couldn't shake it. So, we finished the movie. It's now my favorite horror film.

The next semester, the screenwriting club I was in put on a horror screenplay contest. I continued my horror education. I realized not only was I in love, but I'd been in love this entire time, my whole life. It was like a rom-com. When you realize you want to spend the rest of your life with a genre, you want the rest of your life to start as soon as possible. I was just a girl, standing in front of a genre, asking it to love her. My screenplay won the contest. Horror loved me, too. We met on a bridge at sunrise. We totally made out.

For so long, I thought I couldn't handle horror because I'm too sensitive, because I feel things too intensely, because I'm too anxious, too afraid. But that's exactly why horror is for me. It's a place for me to explore my intensity, my anxieties, my fears, my rage, and so much more.

This is why I love horror. It's a playground where I can unleash my monsters, and they can get their energy out while I sit on a bench watching. For every time I stayed quiet when I wanted to speak up, because I was trying to be good and polite and not be deemed a bitch, horror gives me permission to scream. For every time I deprived myself because I was taught deprivation is a virtue, that want is unbecoming, horror gives me the space to gorge. For every time I was made to feel ashamed of my body, horror allows me the freedom to imagine what it would be like if my body had the power to rip the world apart. For the things I have endured that I cannot bring myself to speak about, horror meets me with no judgment, just hands me a weapon and gives me a wink. A release. Consolation. Understanding.

Plus, it's dairy-free.

Horror Saved
My Life

By Victor LaValle

Victor LaValle's works are personal, and his writing reflects that as he uses his protagonists to take a closer look at the frightening situations he puts them into and allows them to articulate the fear, unease, and terror for his readers. It is as if he inhabits the characters and his readers are looking out through their eyes, experiencing the horror from a very focused view. Because his characters are also marginalized in a variety of ways (e.g., Black men, single women homesteading in Montana, mental institution patients), the disturbing and menacing atmosphere becomes more vivid, immersing readers in the terror inherent in worlds and places with which they may not be familiar. Finally, it is important to note that LaValle also injects moments of dark humor throughout all his stories that work to keep the tone from tipping over into bleaker territory.

Like Rachel Harrison in the previous essay, LaValle looks at his first forays into serious writing, specifically his college years and how he fought horror for (maybe) too long, and yet, it is precisely that conflict and his literary journey that allowed him to find not only his voice but also himself.

Readers new to Victor LaValle should start with The Ballad of Black Tom. *For those who want to try a similar author, I suggest Mariana Enríquez.*

There's a version of this essay where I talk about the ways horror literature and film and comics and TV were formative in my early years. My first love. The one that set me on the path that I'm on today, and what's led me to be a part of this powerful pack of horror writers who are gathered in this book. But I'm not going to talk about that, if only because I feel my story probably wouldn't be that different from so many others gathered here—and heard in so many other places before now. Names that are revered, at least in our little pocket of the literary world, were vital to me: Shirley Jackson, Clive Barker, Peter Straub, and Stephen King; Robert McCammon, John Saul, and Brian Lumley kept me up on plenty of late nights as a kid. I wish there'd been more Black writers, more women, more non-white writers on my list, but I was limited to the mass-market paperbacks I could find on the spinner racks at the local supermarket or pharmacy, and those places were whiter than Vermont in January.

But like I said, I'm not here to talk about the early years. Instead, I'm thinking about the college years. I'd gone through junior high school and high school writing pastiches of my favorite authors—really just ripping off their best short stories and swapping out a location or character names. I had that fire, the enthusiasm; I knew I wanted to be a writer since I was about twelve years old. Showed up to college, did my best, which honestly wasn't all that good, but in my sophomore year I did get into a writing workshop. With all the excitement and ego of a kid who didn't know any better, I turned in a story called "Bleed the Freak." I spent the next week anticipating the rounds of applause I would receive when I stepped into workshop next. Would my professor have spent his free time securing a publishing contract for me? I wondered. Would the other kids in class feel unworthy of looking me in the eye for the rest of the semester?

Some of you reading this might recognize my title. It's the title of a song by a band called Alice in Chains, off their debut album, which had come out the year before. I'd loved it for the way it straddled heavy metal and a kind of horror vibe. And in that song, the chorus repeated the phrase "bleed the freak." I took it, and in my story, I wrote about a group of boys in Queens, New York, who are playing a game of tag, but secretly they've all agreed they are going to kill someone in their group that day. Our main character is the victim. And at the end of the story, they've chased him into a deserted part of Flushing Meadows–Corona Park and have been hurling rocks at him to take him down. He falls into a pit—still in view of the park's famous Unisphere and the towers that were used to such great effect in the first *Men in Black* movie—and they stand over him, each kid holding a rock. And the story ends with the leader of the kids saying that title I swiped from Alice in Chains: "*Bleed the freak.*"

Honestly, I thought it was the coolest shit ever committed to paper.

My classmates and my professor, somehow, did not agree. Generally speaking, they thought it was fine. A few people felt I'd described the park pretty well. They liked my use of a location I understood personally. A few others said they didn't understand why the boys had turned against the main character. Perhaps there was some backstory for the leader that would help explain how he'd become such a damaged human being at an early age. The professor's reaction is totally absent from my memory. Did he write any notes? Did he say anything of value? Complete blank. Considering how desperate I was for attention, for praise, I feel sure I would've held tight to any kind words. I also would've remembered a harsh critique, in the way that all whipped dogs recall their abuse. So I think he offered neither.

But the response I remember most came from an upperclassman. At the end of the workshop, each kid handed over their copy of my story, each one containing some degree of notes. But this upperclassman's copy contained only one note. Sitting all the way at the end. Right after my astoundingly great last line—"*Bleed the freak.*" Right after this, the upperclassman wrote a single word: "*Oooooooooh.*"

How could one word shatter me so badly? Knowing the upperclassman as I did by that point in the semester, I was under no illusion that he meant this word as a sign of deep investment in the story, an indication that he'd been profoundly moved. This dude had never liked anything up till that point in the semester, and he never showed any enthusiasm for the works of others till the end of term. He was just an asshole. Or maybe he felt deeply unhappy with his own life and took it out on me, on all of us. Or maybe his parents had lost their family fortune just the day before. I don't know about him. I only know the effect his response had on me.

I felt silly. I felt stupid for writing that piece. For the first time in my life, I felt ashamed of writing horror.

Now I don't want to oversell the importance of this single moment or give one guy that much power. But I tend to mark that experience—a petty dismissal of something I felt so good about—as the beginning of a certain education I received at school, the central idea being that it's stupid to write horror fiction.

I'd gone to college almost by chance. When I was starting twelfth grade, I'd expected to marry my high school sweetheart and join the Marines. The high school sweetheart part should be obvious. I was in love. The Marines part needs a little more context. I don't come from a military family, and frankly, although a fair number of guys from my neighborhood joined various branches of the service, even more finished high school and got a job and maybe started having kids soon after, and a smaller group of us went to college. When I was in eleventh grade, one guy started coming back around the neighborhood driving a Suzuki Samurai—a compact 4x4—that he'd bought with his own money, earned in the Marines, and when us kids pulled up to the driver's-side window, he'd show us photos of either the guns he'd been using in the service or the women he'd had sex with in a few countries we couldn't spell. In other words, this dude was the greatest advertisement for military service that I had ever seen.

But a buddy of mine demanded I apply to one college before I signed any papers with the Marines. I agreed, but only if he chose the school. He said Cornell University. How he knew that name, I will never guess. For context, he finished college and became an employee at Verizon and a relatively well-known weed dealer in southeast Queens. But he told me to apply and I applied early and I got into that damn school. Soon after my acceptance, my girlfriend broke up with me and the dude with the Suzuki Samurai apparently got into some kind of trouble overseas—I never learned what it was, but I know he never came back to the block—and with that I gave up on getting married at eighteen and joining the Marines. Instead I went to college, very few plans in mind except that I wanted to write. All eggs; one basket.

Then at college, starting with that upperclassman and his single-word critique, I learned that my last remaining dream, to be a great horror writer, was the stupidest dream of all. If I was going to be a *real* writer—respected, award-winning, potentially deserving of a place in the literary canon—then I'd better wise up.

So that's what I did.

———

Of course I would enjoy telling a story about how I always knew myself and always did what I wanted with my writing no matter what the world tried to make me do. But here's the thing: I didn't know much. I'd grown up reading deeply but not widely. I knew the stuff I mentioned earlier, could go deeper and further back to people like Arthur Machen, Algernon Blackwood, Lord Dunsany, and so on. But outside of that one wheelhouse, I knew nothing more than what I'd been taught in high school.

I'd chosen English as my major, which meant I'd better have a broad awareness of the literature that had shaped my genre, but not only my genre. I mentioned the lack of Black writers, women, other non-white folks, but let's add in my lack of regional authors—Southern, Midwestern, Appalachian, Western—to say nothing of writers beyond the shores of the USA. I knew next to nothing. And that embarrassed me. Sometimes shame can be a powerful motivator.

I spent the next few years with writers like Toni Morrison, Herman Melville, Kenzaburō Ōe, Wallace Stegner, Flannery O'Connor, Chinua Achebe, and many more. Like Skynet, I learned at a geometric rate. At least it felt that way. And I read far less horror, or at least far less of the stuff that was expressly packaged as horror (more on that soon). While I never had a professor tell me, explicitly, that horror fiction—or any kind of genre fiction—should be avoided or dismissed, I learned the lesson nonetheless. Even decades later I sometimes try to parse the places where the lesson had been threaded into the lectures, or the syllabi, or the in-class discussions, of the courses I took for my degree. But I can't ever pinpoint the culprit. Nevertheless, like so many cultural lessons, I learned them, in part because they were never overtly expressed.

By the time I graduated college with my English degree (after failing out for half a year; I was a mess in other ways), I'd made the choice to apply to graduate school and got into Columbia University's Writing MFA Program. I'd been happy to get accepted and even happier that I'd be moving back to New York City.

A short summary of that time is that I wrote a lot, met a few truly wonderful and talented friends, finished my first book, found an agent, and, after a somewhat arduous and occasionally humiliating process that is familiar to nearly all writers I know, had my first book published. A collection of realist stories about growing up in Queens. I felt really proud and almost half enjoyed the fact that I'd been published. (This feeling interrupted only by the natural, if indefensible, tendency to pout about why I wasn't paid more for the book or didn't get more reviews and so on. The type of writer bullshit that plagues many of us, regardless of genre.) Then I published a second book, my first novel, this one a realist—if sometimes absurd—story of one family in Queens, many of whose members suffer varying degrees of mental illness (back then I didn't know the term "neurodivergence"), and the more time they spend together the more terrible their lives become. It all culminates in a disaster/shit show that tears the family apart.

Sounds fun, don't it?

Two books down and it was a miracle that I'd published them at all—and was paid a little something for the first and decently for the second. Time to write the third. But as I hunkered down to work, I kept coming up with reasons to step away from the computer. I had a full-time job, and I was also teaching writing classes here and there and trying to date and live in New York. I had no time to write more books! But I'd worked part-time since I was thirteen and was in school, played junior varsity baseball, had a girlfriend, and yet I couldn't stop writing back then. When I was young, I'd felt so eager to write that I stayed up late and snuck in bits of time on the weekend, and even when I wasn't writing, I was *thinking* about writing. What changed?

You're a smart person. You see the bloody writing on the wall. I wish I could say I saw it as quickly as you probably have. What changed is that I'd stopped writing horror. And as a result, I'd lost my connection to the joy that had always been the battery in my back. Writing in and of itself didn't bring me pleasure. Writing horror—that's what made me glow.

At a certain point, I asked myself what I would need to add back into my writing if I wanted to feel that fire burning in my body again. The answer came to me instantly. *Monsters.* If I could write about monsters again, I would find my way back to the pleasures of the page. As I thought about it, I realized my yearning wasn't about any one kind of creature but about the ways that a good monster lets a writer approach all the really great mysteries: What is this world we live in? What lies beyond my comprehension? What tests me in ways that force me to either thrive or be destroyed? What makes me afraid? Monsters, when they're used to their best effect, are just questions that can kill you.

I wrote my third book, a novel called *Big Machine*, about a secret society of Black down-and-outers, former addicts, and criminals who find themselves drawn into a spiritual war that threatens to tear the United States apart. There are monsters in the story; there's a reluctant love story, a reckoning with addiction and the awful things one does to feed their habit, an examination of religious extremism, a story where all the characters are impeccably dressed. I had a fucking blast writing that novel. It's been called many things: speculative fiction, genre-bending literary fiction, slipstream, and more. But I know what it is. It's a horror novel.

And publishing that book marked the start of the best and most lasting part of my writing career. It was when I stopped running and learned—or relearned—to embrace my roots.

And yet, I don't want this essay to seem like the point is that I should never have taken that detour into so many other schools of literature. I am a better writer because of all the other kinds of work I read. More to the point, so many of the books I came to love were just horror novels under a different name. *Beloved* is a ghost story, yes, but the real-world horror of chattel slavery in the United States easily matches some of the harshest realities dreamed up in the world of extreme or Splatterpunk horror. Perhaps, in some ways, it's even more extreme because Morrison didn't make any of American slavery's horrors up. Something similar could be said for Kenzaburō Ōe's *A Personal Matter* or even some of Faulkner's more grueling work. The family tree is grand and it has many branches.

I write this essay now on a plane headed to Nantes, France, where I will participate in a literary festival with other writers from China, Turkey, the United States, and all parts of Europe. Writers of science fiction, fantasy, and horror, gathered in one place. I sit here marveling at where horror has taken me.

But even a plane trip to a part of the world I might otherwise never see falls far short of that greater benefit, feeling plugged into that essential artistic battery: the overwhelming charge I felt as a boy when I read a work of fiction and felt inspired to try to capture that effect on the page so I could transfer it to someone else. That's how horror saved my writing, my career, and my life. It's a debt I'll never repay.

Tales from My Crypt

By Mary SanGiovanni

Mary SanGiovanni has had a long and successful career as a writer and teacher of the most nihilistic branch of horror: cosmic horror. She has taken the sexism and misogyny of cosmic horror's founder, H. P. Lovecraft, head-on in her writing by crafting tales that use the ideas he originated, looking directly into the abyss, forcing readers to contemplate human insignificance in the face of the vast universe, and centering it all around fully fleshed-out women. But she was also forced to take on the misogyny of horror publishing itself in the early days of the twenty-first century, as she was often the only woman in the room and many of her fellow authors and their majority male readers made it clear that they did not always want her there. But she not only persevered, she excelled. SanGiovanni made possible the current generation of women writers, like Hailey Piper, Cynthia Pelayo, and Rachel Harrison, who have been able to center their gender in their terrifying, uncomfortable, and menacing stories, garnering them legions of fans and accolades in the process.

In this essay, SanGiovanni looks closely at her youth, both the real-world terrors and the horror content she consumed, and lands upon one very specific show as the piece of horror that most made her the writer she is today, how it taught her how to tell an effective horror story, and how its influence can still be seen in her work. While this essay is in a similar vein to those written by Harrison and Victor LaValle, SanGiovanni's essay is also positioned here to help prepare you as we approach the end of our Why I Love Horror journey, as her piece contains echoes of all who came before her and *sends us into the final two essays with the hope that all these authors will leave a lasting imprint on the genre itself, even after they are long gone.*

Readers new to Mary SanGiovanni should start with Savage Woods. *For those who want to try a similar author, I suggest Lucy Snyder.*

———————

I've often been asked over the course of my career, "Why horror?" Sometimes it's been phrased, "Why can't you write something nice and cute and happy?" or even "Why can't you write something that makes money?" Ultimately, though, the question—or, perhaps, concern—on the minds of folks who don't see themselves as fans of horror is why anyone would knowingly, willingly, immerse themselves in a genre that seems to revel in the worst and most terrifying parts of nightmares, the ugliest truths, the most shocking indifference, and the most heartbreaking tragedy. Further, why would someone who has an ounce of decency manufacture more of that and foist it upon the world?

It's a valid enough question, I guess, on the surface. It usually tells me that the questioner doesn't really know much, if anything, about the genre and its myriad subgenres and styles, nor has said person read the finest of its treatments of multiple subject matters, themes, and subtexts. That isn't a criticism. There are some people for whom the necessary psychological elements of survival include drawing a distinct line in the sand of reality and then grounding themselves on one side of it. They may not have the stomach for dread or horror, nor do they enjoy coasting the crest of terror at its height, even vicariously through safe methods like media. For them, escapism isn't about catharsis or even exploration of the unknown. They want the warm-fuzzy feels, as they say. No one can really fault them for that.

But I am not that kind of girl.

I've been blessed with a long career in supernatural horror, particularly cosmic horror, which is often viewed as the pinnacle of nihilism and the absolute antithesis of the goals and aims of the people I just described above. If one fears pain, death, loss, loneliness, insanity . . . then cosmic horror does you one better. It postulates that there are fates even worse than death and that maybe, just maybe, there are no happy endings—not in this world, and not in the next, either.

And yet, despite being an optimist by nature, I find this freeing. To me, there is limitless possibility in this kind of literature—the eternal questions of "What if?" and "What else?" echoed into multiple universes . . . and the response from the darkest fathoms of the cosmos: "Everything . . . and nothing."

But I'm getting ahead of myself. I titled this essay "Tales from My Crypt" for a reason, and I should probably start a ways back if I am to answer why I proudly, unabashedly, and sanely love horror.

When I was a child, I was a voracious reader. I was also a huge fan of movies as well as video and computer games. I have always been drawn to those of the speculative variety—that delightful triad of horror, fantasy, and science fiction. I grew up in a typical middle-class New Jersey suburb in the '80s, playing *Haunted House* and *Cosmic Ark* on the Atari and *Tass Times in Tonetown* and the *King's Quest* games on the PC. My parents were both college-educated, and my father had a good job in industry publishing. I was the oldest, so when I was of an age to watch over my sisters, my mom went back to work part-time. My sisters and I would come home after school, change clothes (we went to a Catholic school and had to wear uniforms, which I loathed), have a snack, and do our homework.

Around 4:30, *Scooby-Doo* was on (in syndication). That was my first real foray into anything macabre, and I loved it. I loved everything about it: the tease of something supernatural and scary, the nebulous threat of the monster "getting" someone (even though the monster always turned out to be a human in a mask), and the logic that went into solving crimes. As I have grown, so has the franchise, changing and evolving into something kids of today might relate to better. But the *Scooby-Doo* that I remember typified that uninhibited and unapologetic post-hippie generation of young people traveling the country and having adventures. There was probably more to it than I caught back then—the implication that Fred and Daphne were probably hooking up and that Shaggy and Scooby were probably getting high in the Mystery Machine between run-ins with ghosts—but I was a really little kid then, and I didn't pick up on that so much as the idea that a group of young people were facing down the things they were most terrified of and using their wits to outsmart those things. They were helping people. In essence, they were helping me and all the other little kids who were almost two decades behind them and scared of . . . well, everything.

See, we little kids wouldn't ever really know the feeling of being completely free of fear. We were the tail end of the Gen-X latchkey-kid lifestyle, raised somewhere between absent-parenting and helicopter-parenting styles. We were essentially taught that despite all the escapist promises—the Care Bears, Barbie, My Little Pony, *Pac-Man, Dungeons & Dragons*, Tang, and the fantastic and wonderful *Heavy Metal*–style body-builder-born fantasy of the '80s that could only have been made and fully appreciated in that decade—we were in constant danger.

Our generation was fed on fears that somehow seemed as if they were only then being discovered or finally being recognized. Our childhood sanctuaries and bastions of escape, our cartoons and children's shows, even some of our Jim Henson Muppets, were violent, with familial, societal, and existential terror stoked by *The NeverEnding Story*, *The Last Unicorn*, *The Secret of NIMH*, *Watership Down*, and *The Dark Crystal*. We had a new "war" on drugs, the horrors of which were drilled into us as early as third grade. We were too little then to have an inkling that the very people scaring us with stories of drug addiction and overdose were the ones sanctioning its trafficking into the country to help fund *other* people in a faraway place to stop something called communism, a big nebulous bad in and of itself that, if left unchecked, would threaten the American way of life. There was the Cuban missile crisis and the Cold War, something grown-ups talked about over our heads, something they indicated might well end with bombs big enough to vaporize huge swaths of the planet. There was stranger danger seemingly at every street corner, in every stairwell. Back then, it seemed the deadliest thing we could do was accept a ride from a stranger; hitchhiking, a staple of transportation for the big kids who came before us, was now a surefire ticket to rape, torture, and murder. There were no more freewheeling jaunts around the country having adventures like the *Scooby-Doo* gang, because we had entered the age of serial killers. We had kidnappings at Chuck E. Cheese, so many that they closed the chain in my area for decades. Hell, we even had talks on the dangers of lightning and gas explosions and disappointing Smokey Bear by setting forest fires. We now had stricter laws on drunk driving and wearing seat belts. We still had urban legends and campfire stories, too, the creepypastas of the time; we feared razor blades in Halloween candy and hook-handed murderers and rapists in the back seats of cars. Before we were even really aware of what sex was, we were warned of the dangers of free love and hooking up with a new person every week, like in *Three's Company*, because of that new and terrible illness called AIDS. And of course, remember, I went to Catholic school. There was no shortage of sin and failure and guilt and the Devil and demons and Hell.

Despite all this, or maybe because of it, there was an innocent appreciation of the fantastical that seemed to surge in media. I don't know if it was the cocaine or the sharp disparity in economic classes. I don't know if it was the need to escape impending nuclear war or the boom of fantasy in books, movies, and video games. I don't know if it was the sharp dissonance and discontent inherent in putting all these things together. But some of that innocence, that naive belief in God and country of past generations, was lost. People say that it was the '60s that killed it, with the Vietnam War, with race riots and protests and hippie psychos like Charles Manson and their cults, but I disagree. I think America tried, as a country, to hold on to its childhood a little longer, to affectionately indulge the dad joke, to cheer the fluffy-haired, surf-tanned, pop-collared frat boy and pretty, Aqua Netted, shoulder-padded good girl next door they thought had promise. The '80s were our country's preteen phase, before the full onset of the jaded, sullen teenage decade of the '90s.

But even that young, we'd seen some shit.

While all this weight was heaped on the shoulders of the children who would, in the sci-fi far future of 2024, inherit the earth, right there at the end of the '80s, a new horror anthology series based on EC Comics aired called *Tales from the Crypt*.

It gleefully embraced all the naughtiness and dangerous behavior we were told to avoid at all costs, and it absolutely provided unfettered access to a world beyond ours. And there was a simple message: bad will find a way to reclaim its own. It promised that even the helpless, the weak, the blindly trusting, the duped—those who were hampered and held down by fear—could take control, have power, exact revenge, and, finally, be free of all fear. In those stories, the supernatural reigned, for better or worse, and the universe, a bigger thing than suburban New Jersey or even America, would see that things are eventually put right.

I'm sure some episodes hold up better than others, but I have a soft spot and a nostalgic love for this show. It ran seven seasons, and I think I've seen nearly every single episode, many of them multiple times. I learned some of the most rudimentary aspects of horror writing from the simple revenge formula contained therein, and something of the baser nature of humanity. Here were moral shades of gray in vivid color, characters with adult needs and desires. Universal fears, both timely and immortal, emerged from their nether places in gruesome detail. Here, most certainly, there be monsters—not the kind in the mask, but real ones, both natural and supernatural. And sometimes, the monsters won.

Humor and the grotesque made entertaining, if discomforting, bedfellows. Just when you felt like you were in on the secret or the joke, a stab of violence or gore or the unexpected would thrill you from beyond the grave or from one of the dark and secret places of the earth . . . or outside of it.

See, *Tales from the Crypt*—and horror in general—made those dark, secret, thrilling places somehow seem more possible, more versatile, more accessible. Further, it promised that the absolute freedom in those places could be mine for a time—freedom from the real-world fears of everyday life and also from the bounds of reality itself.

That appealed to me, this sexy, daring, disturbing, amusing, scary array of stories detailing the misfortunes of those who ran afoul of forces they didn't, couldn't, or wouldn't understand or respect. I found my reading, movie, and video/computer game tastes slowly drifting away from high fantasy (which I still love and always will) toward the darker and deadlier, the more shocking and terrifying. There was freedom in those dark places, the scary kind like despair and resignation and the triumphant kind like victory and acceptance. For the first time, I loved the adrenaline high of being scared and the acceptance that the dark existed but could possibly be overcome. I loved the transformative effect on characters, many of them becoming better than their former selves, using wits and bravery, evolving into resilient or self-sacrificing heroes. I loved those atmospheric moments that would build to some revelation of powerful and frightening importance.

Most of all, I loved the fluidity and endless possibility inherent in a genre that sought to counter the rules of a reality restricted by fear.

That—*that right there*—is what I fell in love with about horror.

Some people will tell you that the only way to live is to impose a form and order to things, to insist on a staunch and unwavering definition of reality, to establish and hold to a clear-cut notion of what is right and wrong, to see justice served, and, possibly, to compel those who don't agree to form a very good relationship with a therapist.

Again, I tell you, I am not that kind of girl.

I learned from morbid tales that one of the best parts of adult life is its fluidity, its flexibility. The unseen world beyond the veil is never as far away as we think. Magic and mystery and adventure aren't just for children; they are a real part of the world around us . . . if you know where to look.

And look I did. I found Stephen King, Ray Bradbury, Clive Barker, Ramsey Campbell, Charles L. Grant, Peter Straub, Arthur Machen, Clark Ashton Smith, Gary Braunbeck, and Douglas Clegg.

I also found H. P. Lovecraft. Say what you will (and rightfully so) about the man's abhorrent views on race, but he did something few in this industry ever have or will manage to accomplish: he transcended writing fiction and created a new mythology, complete with a bible of sorts and a pantheon of gods that have bled so deeply into pop culture and the occult as to have become legend.

And that was when I fell in love with horror all over again. Because I am *that* kind of girl.

In this life, limited as it is, we only have our legacy, which is not what we leave behind but what mark we make on the world. I mean, it is not our children, but how our children remember us. It's not the books we wrote, but how they made readers feel and what they helped readers get through. It's not the kind works we did or the money we donated or the little words and deeds, but the support they afforded people to embrace a second wind and take another chance.

I hope to accomplish those things: to have my children grow up feeling loved and supported and understood because I was there for them. To have my husband and my friends and loved ones remember a kindness or a smile when they think of me. To have readers remember that, for a time, what I wrote was more than a book in their hands, but a moment of unlimited possibility of other worlds, an existence bigger and more everlasting than humanity, full of darkness and promise and light . . . and absolute freedom.

When the sound of me is silenced by dirt and stone above me, I hope my voice can go on. And I would be honored to have that voice join the others in the endless and fantastic halls of the genre I love.

Of Men and Monsters

By David Demchuk

David Demchuk is a Canadian author who has been vocal about how his love of horror stems from its ability to be a place from which he can directly explore and address his queerness, disability, and eastern European heritage. Since his work quite consciously looks at otherness head-on, intense unease penetrates his stories even before the monsters arrive, setting the stage for a battle of horrors both real and supernatural. Of note, Demchuk's work can also be experimental in nature, from actively retelling well-known dark tales to employing an epistolary style to metafiction; however, the complicated style of his work is always underpinned by his embracing of horror's history and an appreciation for the genre's traditions and the power horror holds over humanity.

Demchuk's essay is our penultimate entry, and it is positioned here because he helps us transition from the previous sixteen essays, which told us why the authors each love horror. Instead, he proceeds to show us, with a story similar to the ones he was told as a kid, how a horror story connects him to his fascination with monsters. It is a proof of concept for this entire endeavor, as he brings us closer to the end of our journey with a reminder that horror can nourish the soul.

Readers new to David Demchuk should start with RED X. For those who want to try a similar author, I suggest John Darnielle.

———

I have written many times about my love of horror as a place to express and explore my queerness and disability, and my fascination with monstrosity as an idea we see in horror specifically and in our culture generally: the othering of those who are different, the desire to persecute and destroy the unfamiliar and uncomprehended. But more than this, my love of horror and my fascination with monsters are deeply connected to the stories I was told as a child or that I overheard when my family members thought I was not listening.

I would like to start by telling one of these stories. It is a story of war, of grief and loss, of men and monsters. It is a horror story, the kind I have always loved to hear and that I love to tell. I would hear tales like this from my uncle, whispered as though they were dark incantations, and he heard them from my grandfather. My father would never tell me such things. He would only shake his head and say, "You never know what you call upon when you tell such stories as these."

The story begins in a land, a disputed land, that is riven by famine and destruction and death. There have been many such lands, and we know of lands like these today. We begin with a father and two young sons, hungry and aching and cold, wandering among the rubble where hospitals, schools, and homes once stood. The father's leg is injured. He struggles to walk, can barely stand. There is no food. There has not been for days. There is no water. The father and sons have reached what used to be a street teeming with merchants and hawkers, women and children. Now, there is no one. The air is heavy with rot and decay, the sun is sharp and unsparing. All is still and silent except for a wind that scrapes the skin like a blade and the distant thud and rumble of explosions. You know of places like these, you have seen them. No one survives for long unless they keep moving, but the two boys are tired, they can walk no farther, and the father cannot lift and carry them both. He stops at what once was a plaza where three streets intersected. He scans the ruins frantically, and he spies a hole in the cobbled ground beside what used to be a library, with room enough for the three of them to slip inside, if only for an hour or two, perhaps until dusk. The stench from the hole is particularly strong, but it is dark inside, and no doubt cooler than the dirt and dust and stones that surround them. He leads them to the hole, helps them slide in—the older first and then the younger—and then he follows after them into the wound in the ground. Battered old books and torn pages are scattered inside. Starving rodents scurry down in the darkness. The hole itself feels like something alive.

As I say, this is a story more whispered than told, as it has a power that cannot be directed, cannot be contained. You fire it into the air and you cannot know where it will land. It is a horror story. It contains horrors and it creates horrors. It places horrors in the mind. It is a dark lens through which we see our world, our lives, and we tremble at the sight. Why am I drawn to these stories? Why do I collect them and repeat them, and create such stories of my own? In large part it is because they tell uncomfortable truths. There is a ruthlessness in these tales. They slice like a knife that cuts two ways, a knife with a blade for a handle that cuts as deeply into the teller as the listener. In an odd way, their unsparing honesty provides a consolation.

Now, you might ask about the father's wife, the mother of the two boys. She was with them in the ruins of the school where a dozen other people sheltered, where they were directed to go because it was said to be safe, although nothing was safe and had not been for weeks. They heard a clutch of soldiers approach, heard them murmuring in their language, and then the scraping clicking of metal as they prepared to fire on the school and kill its inhabitants. But something went wrong. One of the weapons exploded as the soldiers handled it, shredding them and setting them afire. Those sheltering inside the school screamed and ran out in all directions, fearing they were next, and in the confusion the father's wife was separated and carried off by the other survivors. More explosions, more screams, but the father could not look back, he could only pull his sons away from the blasts and crouch and scuttle out of harm's way. So now the father and the two boys were alone with no way to know if the mother was alive and safe, or if she was not.

If you seek out these stories, the way that I do, you come to see patterns in the way they are told, in how they unfold gently and carefully, moment by moment, like those rare flowers that bloom in the evening when the waking world comes to rest. You see the way the language curls and entwines, pulling the listener closer to the story's dark heart, and you see how that dark heart reveals itself, exposes itself to the listener: a gift, a jewel, a treasure. You see how the stories of others—of strangers, of people and creatures from other lands and other times—become your own story, a story you know as if you wrote it, as if you lived it yourself.

In this story, the two boys sleep in the dark, putrid mouth that was opened in the side of the library, and their father sits just inside the opening and watches over them. As he does so, he receives three visitors. These visitors are phantoms, revenants, creatures. They are fearsome, frightful, and yet they are to be pitied. They were once human, and the tatters of humanity still cling to them, making one believe for a moment—a moment too long—that they are more human than not. When we talk of monsters in stories like these, we are almost always speaking of metaphors: representations of forces beyond our control or understanding, unknowable aspects of our loved ones or of strangers, or the shadow sides and dark secrets we conceal within ourselves. Grief, fury, shame, desolation. We have all felt these things, and they have all threatened to consume us. Every fairy tale, even the most benign and remote, is a tale of today—or else we would not tell it.

There are many versions of this story I am telling, and each is different until this moment—different lands, different times, different wars, sometimes three friends or brothers, sometimes a mother and two daughters—but from this moment forward, all versions of the story are the same.

The sun sets. Day turns to dusk turns to night, and the stars peer down onto the ruined city from the vast black sky. The father nods off to the sound of his children's gentle snoring, then startles awake as a figure approaches, shuffling and hobbling, faint clouds of dust rising in its wake. As it draws closer, the father sees scorched flayed flesh, crooked limbs, missing fingers, remnants of clothing. This was once a soldier, he realizes, one of those caught in the explosion outside the school. But how can he be alive? What is he, if he is not?

"Hear me," croaks the figure. "I have come to seek your forgiveness. Until you grant it, I cannot rest."

The father cannot believe his ears. "Forgive you?" he cries. "You want that I should forgive you? For the destruction you have brought to my family and to my people? I am one person among thousands who have been devastated by this war. Forgiveness is not within my power. Leave us. I pray you never find peace."

"Your sons sleep at your feet," the figure says, reaching for the father. "Think of them and all that they have endured. Death is close to us all this night. Wake them and come with me. I cannot undo what has been done, but I can lead you out of this place to one where you will be safe and cared for. Take my hand and release me from this burden. I cannot carry it for all eternity."

"It is a choice you made in life, and now in death you face the consequence," the father says. "We are safer here than we would ever be with you. Take back your hand, your pleas for pity, and go. Never again speak of my sons. May your children always be lost to you, may you crawl blind and broken through a vast and endless darkness. Be forever damned, and be gone."

A shiver runs through the figure, revealing something vile and feral within him. "You will regret your words," he growls, and like a swirl of smoke he vanishes.

Even now, as I tell this story, I am chilled by each unsettling detail. I feel the father's anger but also the soldier's sorrow, and I fear for the children asleep in their shallow resting place. What manner of monster is this that has cloaked itself in a shambling wraith, and how can it be dispelled so easily? A grim, insistent sense of dread throbs within you. Whatever the season in which this story is told, whatever the day or the hour, you cannot help but wish for a blanket to pull up to your chin or for a hot cup of tea to warm your bones.

After the figure vanishes, the father turns his attention to his sleeping sons. He fears he might have woken them, but they are deep in their dreams, no doubt exhausted from the journey. In the distance, there are more explosions, more cries of terror, and then an uneasy silence. After a moment, the father hears something from below, from deeper inside the hole that is their shelter. He kneels down and listens closer, careful not to disturb the boys. The younger one is restless, it seems, scraping his foot back and forth in the dirt, muttering things the father cannot quite hear. The father runs his hand across the boy's head, through his fine thin hair. The boy calms and quiets under his soothing touch. The father looks down, sees a single page from an unknown book clutched in the child's hand. He carefully slips it out from between the boy's fingers and examines it: a list of landmarks, architects, and dates. All gone now, this is certain. Above the list, a fine line drawing of the skyline of the city that is no more. The father crumples the page, tosses it aside, then leans back and resumes his vigil. The earth turns imperceptibly with each passing moment. The time soon comes for the second visitor.

Though the first figure's arrival startled the father, this second one feels like an inevitability. He now knows, as we do, that this night's passage is a test, a trial, that can only end at dawn. This figure is draped from head to toe, its face veiled as it moves gravely and gracefully toward him. A mourning woman, is what the father thinks—or is the gauzy fabric that envelops her a shroud? He realizes from her gait that he knows this woman, and this feeling grips his heart as she lowers the drape from across her face. It is his wife—but how could this be true? And if it is not his wife, the mother of his sons, then who or what could it be?

"My husband," she says, "I have found you. Are the children with you? Bring them to me. Stand up from your hiding place and take me in your arms."

"Our sons are sleeping down here where it is cool and sheltered. And I am injured, my leg will not support me. How is it that you have found us, here in the darkness, so far from where we lost you?"

"I pulled away from the confusion of the crowd and spied you from afar, but I had to keep myself in the shadows," she replies. There is something uncanny about her, something not quite right. "But look at you, how weak you are. If you cannot walk, how will you care for our sons? How will you lead them out of this place? I am strong and can move swiftly." She reaches out her arms to him. "Wake them and give them to me. I will send help for you when I can."

"It would be wiser to let them rest with me, here where they are hidden," the father answers, his eyes narrowing. His wife would never suggest that he be left behind. "Instead, you should find us some food and water, and bring them back for us to share. Then we can all leave together in the hour before sunrise. You may be strong and swift alone, but our greatest strength is with each other. If you are who you say you are."

The woman's lip curls in contempt, exposing an unusually sharp incisor. "You will wish you had chosen differently," she sneers.

Like the visitor before her, a shudder courses through her from head to toe, unmasking something inhuman and depraved, and with a hiss and a snarl she vanishes. As she does so, the stench from the mouth in the earth grows stronger: sulfuric, metallic, gaseous. It stings his eyes and scours his lungs. It is as if the bowels of Hell have ruptured beneath them. The father can barely keep his eyes open. His leg is swollen, his body aches, his brow is fevered. His sons are still and silent. The older wanted to be a teacher or a doctor. The younger wanted to fly among the stars. What kind of life could they ever hope for now?

Listening to stories like this as a child, I wondered if such things had happened to my own father or uncle or grandfather, if they had suffered through war and famine, if they had been visited by devils offering tests and temptations. Would the same things happen to me, and would I be prepared if they did? I had been frightened, and thrilled, by stories of wicked witches and sleeping princesses, poisoned apples and lost slippers and pumpkin coaches and helpful woodland creatures. But I thought of these as tales for babies: the events they described could not have happened to anyone in my family, and they would never happen to me. My uncle told his stories as if they were part of his past, irrefutable and inescapable, and within them all our families' fates were entwined. Each was a shard of a shattered mirror in which I could see a fragment of myself. Piece by piece, they helped me see the larger whole.

There is one last visitor. This figure emerges as if from the dust itself, just as the night has turned toward morning, with the faintest, gentlest light brushing the horizon's edge. The father hears the soft footfalls, opens his eyes, lifts his head from the ground, and watches as the figure approaches. It is a man, stepping forward with one leg, pulling his other along in an awkward, unpleasant rhythm. The father knows at once why this figure frightens him more than the others. He is looking at himself.

"The night is nearly done," the figure says as he draws closer. The father feels like he is staring into a mirror. "The soldiers will soon descend upon this place in search of any survivors. They will kill without hesitation. Come with me now, while you still can walk, and we will leave this place together."

"You want me to come with you alone? Without my sons?" The father is incredulous. "How can you ask such a thing?"

"Your sons are already dead," the figure says. "The fumes from beneath the building overtook them in the night. They lived their last moments in peaceful dreams of a world beyond their grasp."

Wild with pain and terror, the father rushes down to his sons, shakes them and strikes them and tries to wake them, all in vain. The figure spoke the truth. His children are gone. His wife is gone. He has nothing and no one, except himself. The figure kneels down and reaches for him, as the other figures did. "We have no time to grieve. The first stars have started to fade from the sky. Let me lift you up and help you out of here."

"Don't you see? I cannot leave," the father says. "Without my wife, my sons, my home, there is no life left for me. If I must die, then I will die here with my arms around my children. If you truly wish to help me, lift me up into the world of dreams and let me breathe my last."

The figure shakes his head and stands, and looks out to the east as the first light of dawn streaks the sky. He holds up a hand, and a searing, screeching sound fills the air. The remains of the building above the father's head explode, closing the mouth in the ground and burying him in the rubble. Another blast, and another, and the father lives no more.

Across what is left of the street, the first two figures stand in the night's last shadows, patiently waiting for the third to join them. This is but one of the thousands of wars they have scavenged over the centuries. Once together, they will shed their false skins and walk out into the ruined city, looking for other souls to feed on. They will not go hungry for long.

You never know what you call upon when you tell such stories as these. They can carry you thousands of miles in the time it takes to shed a tear, they can make you taste the pain and suffering of strangers, they can show you the glistening muscular hearts of people you were raised to hate. They can open wounds beneath the skin, and only you will know they are there. These stories nourish you with brutal unwanted truths, laced with shards of glinting glass, leaving you with a mouthful of blood and dust. Other children would retreat to their beds in fear, but I did not and I will not.

Art, we are told, cannot stop missiles, cannot cool the burning phosphorus, cannot make the drones drop from the skies. It cannot bring back the dead. But where we tell our truths, where we recite the names, they cannot say they never heard them. They cannot say they never knew. They cannot say that we approved, that we forgive. I too enjoy my share of pleasant songs, pretty landscapes, quiet walks by the untroubled sea. I too can turn away, but not for long. In the end, I come back to where I will always be: in the hallway, on the floor, hours past my bedtime, my blanket clutched close, soft blue flannel edged in satin, listening as my uncle speaks, in the dark where none can see me, just outside the kitchen door.

Why Horror

By Stephen Graham Jones

It is no exaggeration to say that Stephen Graham Jones is the strongest voice of our current generation of horror authors. Yes, he has the most literary awards. Yes, he is extremely prolific. Yes, his work has explored just about every sub-genre, monster type, and trope. Yes, he has a PhD and, as a university professor, is training the next generation of writers. But it is more than that. Jones uses horror to force readers to look at truth in the world and in themselves. As a Blackfeet, he also leverages his Native perspective to take a hard look at America itself. His evocative language, strong characterization, inventive storylines, and ability to make every detail matter draw readers in and keep them there even as things go from uneasy to unnerving to all-out disaster. His tales can be gruesome, and terrible things will happen; however, disturbing situations and scenes of bloody carnage are always balanced out by thought-provoking insight and emotionally resonant, perfectly rendered endings noted for their heartfelt beauty. The result is in equal measures comforting and unsettling, and the entire genre is elevated because of what Jones brings to his work.

Therefore, it should come as no surprise that Jones is here to present this book's final argument, a list enumerating his reasons for "why horror," from a perspective both laser focused on himself and broadly expanded to include the entire history of humanity. Like his fiction, this essay is graceful, immersive, original, and beautiful, written with his unique narrative cadence, but it is also undeniably terrifying. Horror is inescapable because it is in our DNA. Jones reminds us of this, uniting the entire anthology, and reminding all why they picked up this book in the first place.

Readers new to Stephen Graham Jones should start with The Only Good Indians. *For those who want to try a similar author, I suggest Andy Davidson.*

———

Because I like to eat ketchup. The problem with that, though, it's . . . you guessed it: occasional red drips down the front of my shirt. This was a problem for a while, but then I figured out that I could simply cut those bothersome ketchup stains out of whatever shirt I was wearing and then surreptitiously place little squares of electrical tape on my skin *under* that hole, effectively hiding what I'd done. Only problem with that was I would always jump-scare myself at the end of the day when I peeled that shirt off and had these little black squares on my chest and stomach. But then a more obvious solution presented itself: only wearing black or at least black-adjacent T-shirts. And, because I move in horror circles, with horror people, at horror conventions, in the horror aisle of bookstores, I don't stand out—we're *all* wearing black T-shirts, aren't we? If not on our bodies, then in our hearts. So, why horror? Because of what I wear.

Because I'm confident horror's the oldest genre. So, getting to write it, I feel like I'm sort of going back to the Source. Think about it: a hunting party in Paleolithic times comes back all scratched up and dehydrated and traumatized after nine days gone, and instead of having enough meat to make it all the way through the coming winter, they only have enough meat to maybe eke their band through a few more days. Which isn't necessarily enough to garner them censure or even punishment—hunting's never a sure thing, and any meat's better than no meat at all—but, all the same, they can hear the stomachs rumbling around the campfire that night. This hunting party can see the hollowness in the eyes of the people they care for, and they want to explain themselves, they want to tell them why they didn't build a sledge and domesticate some horses and drag a whole woolly mammoth home. So one of them waits for the right quiet moment, stares deep and meaningfully into the flames, breathes in so everyone knows to listen, and starts in muttering about the . . . the *monster* they encountered three valleys over. The hunting party was stalking this small herd, doing everything right, when they realized they were being stalked. At first it was just a feeling, then it was a sound, then it was—was that breathing they were hearing? And, in telling this story, this hunter has looked up from the fire to lock eyes with listener after listener. And, at just the right moment, this hunter rises, the flames underlighting their face, haunting their features up. And then, whispering about how the monster was there, behind that wall of grass, then *there*, just past that tree, they start to stalk around the fire, the shadows dancing, their posture menacing and animalistic—*hungry*. It's the kind of performance that makes the people seated around this fire hug themselves, and maybe scoot closer to whoever's beside them, and not look away from this hunter even for an instant. Not just because they've got the story, but because they've touched the horror themselves and are maybe infected with it now. You never know. Horror, it's been with us since the very beginning. Getting to be that person who made it back from three valleys over not with meat but with a story . . . that's stepping into a long line of storytellers. It's the highest honor.

Because it makes us human. We spent some six million years pulling ourselves together on the savanna. Over those six million years, we were trading trees for a more ground-bound way of life, meaning we no longer needed the upper body strength that was good both for hanging from tree limbs *and* for self-defense. When we got omnivorous, that meant our teeth had to be multipurpose, couldn't be sharp and scary anymore. When we needed to sweat in order to run prey down in the heat of the day when that prey was at a disadvantage, we lost our fur, which had previously been pretty good camouflage. On and on like this, we lost attribute after attribute that could help us survive in tooth-and-claw land. And the hungry things patrolling these grasslands, they definitely took note of this. Until our big brains started giving us language to coordinate defensive strategies, until we figured out to throw rocks and use fire as a weapon, until we knew to build structures to keep the hungry things at bay, until we had pointy-jabby-shooty things . . . we were pretty much the chicken nuggets of the savanna, weren't we? What this means is that every darkness, every next step, every time the sky yawned open above us—eagles were a terror to our evolving selves—we had to be on not just high alert, but the highest alert. We *knew* the chicken nuggets we were. We *knew* there were slavering teeth waiting for us every moment of our lives. And that kind of certainty, if it doesn't get hardwired into us, then . . . then we're not vigilant enough, we all get eaten, we don't make it through enough generations and millennia to learn how to sharpen sticks into spears. What this means is that monsters, they're built into us at an instinctual level. They're an essential part of what makes us human. But? In today's world, where we shine lights into all the corners and disinfect all the surfaces, where we remove all the bitey things from our daily existence, we don't feel the immediate threat or even presence of those slavering teeth anymore, do we? There are other very real and pressing concerns, for sure. But we're no longer that concerned about being actually digested by something we never had a chance against. Trick is, though, we *need* that. That spike of terror, of certainty, that reminder that we're not the apex anything, it's what keeps us human. If we ever forget the chicken nuggets we most definitely are, then . . . then we're not quite human. Horror, what it can do is give the contemporary world those slavering teeth. Horror can not just remind us that we're human, but it can instill our chicken-nugget nature back into us, so that we're watching the sky again, so that we're listening with all we have around the next corner. Because you never know, do you? Why horror? Because it keeps us never knowing, it keeps us uncertain, it keeps us nervous. It keeps us human.

Because the stakes are always, from the get-go, so high. Even in stories where we don't encounter the big bad until, say, the last third. Just the fact that this is on the horror *shelf*, that signals to us that the stakes here, they're life and death, and maybe even worse than that—the *soul* can be at stake, *reality* can be at stake, *existence* can be at stake. In horror, things matter, and they usually matter immediately. It's very much like an opera in that way. Or, really, it's very much like being a teenager, isn't it? Your emotions are turned up to 11 from the first moment you open your eyes in the morning. You don't know what's going to happen or why, but your response is probably going to be overblown in this opera you didn't even ask to be involved in. And, while high school maybe isn't always the most pleasant time, as daily life's this out-of-control ride that never ends, it is nice to be moving through a space where everything *matters*, isn't it? And it doesn't only matter, but it matters a lot—the stakes are intimidatingly high. In his craft book *The Triggering Town*, Richard Hugo says that the best material is as close as you can get to the sentimental and melodramatic without quite crossing over into that space. Horror is forever balancing on that line of "too much." And that's what makes it so fun. Like Springsteen says when the mom in his song warns him about staring too long at the sun: "But, Momma, that's where the fun is." It's the same in horror. And that's a big reason I'll never be able to stay away from it. It's the main reason I don't even try to stay away.

Because when you get tired of a character, you can cut their head off. Or eviscerate them. Feed them into an upturned lawn mower. Sic a werewolf on them. There's endless ways to wipe them off the page, and every one of those ways only makes the story better, more intense.

Because horror lays dark eggs in the audience's head that don't hatch until two in the morning. When you read or watch something that's unsettling, that has sticky imagery, that's upending what you thought your moral sensibilities were, you defend against that by looking for the zipper running down this monster's back, don't you? It's just self-preservation—*sleep* preservation. In fiction, that zipper can be a poorly executed line, a misspelled word, an inaccuracy that pulls the whole facade down. On a screen, that zipper can be wooden dialogue, poorly composed shots, a boom mic hanging over a character's head. And, in both of these, it can be an *actual* zipper too, can't it? Whatever "zipper" means to you—whatever you think it is that's keeping you safe while engaging this scary story—that's great for the moment, sure. You don't throw the book across the room. You don't run from the theater hiding your eyes and covering your ears. But? Come two in the morning, when you're not really expecting it, when you feel safe, like you got through that experience . . . that's when it comes back for you, doesn't it? That's when these particular dark eggs hatch. You're walking down the empty hallway for a glass of water. You're clacking through a cavernous parking garage. And you become aware of the silence around you in a different way. You maybe even hear a zipper coming down out in that great darkness, and you close your eyes and your heart against it, sure. It's too late, though. That was a costume, you were right. But . . . now that that costume's falling away, what's left standing there? It's your worst fears, exposed. And they're coming for you. And, worse than that, you invited them in—you told some big evil chicken they could play with your insides, and we did. Oh, did we ever. What's not to love about that?

Because of the community. I challenge anyone out there to find a more supportive group of people than horror fans. We all love our chosen genre enough that just moving among other people with that same wonderful infection, we'll stay in the lobby all night, talking about this novel, that film—this one scare that still lights us up all these years later. And the horror community seems to understand that a win for one of us is a win for all of us, in that horror's now, because of this particular win, gone wider, gotten bigger, is drawing in people who maybe never would have called themselves horror fans before. We're always welcoming, though, that's a thing about this horror tribe, these Halloween people. We've all spent so long banished from polite society that we've sort of formed our own group out here at the edge of things, and what we've found out here away from the light is solidarity. But it feels like faith, doesn't it? We defend what we believe in, but not by taking down whatever other genres are out there. Those other genres thrive—fine, wonderful, keep doing that. We're going to keep pulling these blood gags out here at our nightmare carnival, though, if you don't mind. Or, I guess, even if you do mind. And, if it's cool with all y'all other genres, we might incorporate a little of your romance into our horror? Maybe some action and adventure. A bit of that crime and mystery? Some of those oh-so-fine sentences? Or maybe we set the scary stuff in your Old West town. Maybe we take it to the moon. Horror, one of the great things about it is that it can happen anywhere—any setting, any era, any medium, any genre. All you need is a character with something to lose. Maybe a world that thinks things are clicking along just fine. Horror's a happy face sticker that adheres to anything. Just . . . that sticky stuff on the back, maybe don't look too closely at it? It's tacky like it should be, yeah, like it needs to be if the sticker's going to work, but . . . that stickiness, it might be a bit red. With all the bits of ourselves we bleed out in order to get the good stuff down on the page.

Because in the darkness, even a speck of light is bright. Another way to say this is that I don't write horror for the darkness. I write it for the good moments—for the heart, for the hope, for the chance of winning, no matter how distant and unlikely, no matter the cost. But you can't have those good moments without a long, torturous grind through the badness—doesn't the good taste better after having had to suffer through the bad? Isn't this why the salad precedes the meal? But I'd rather see a single small daisy out in a bleak, frozen landscape than a whole field of wildflowers thriving. To me, that one daisy, it's a fighter, it's a striver, it's had to struggle so hard to be where it is. I believe in that one daisy way out there more than I believe in that carpet of splashy colors sighing back and forth in the breeze by the easy water source, with the sun always shining down, and signs telling hikers not to trample all this prettiness, please. No, give me that one brave flower out there that doesn't even know how to bow its head, that doesn't know what surrender *is*. Even if it doesn't make it through the winter, it tried, didn't it? To me, that's what horror's about: the trying, the fighting, the hope.

Because you never know the ending. Horror stories, they can end any which way, can't they? They're not all tragic and despondent, they're not all celebratory and victorious. Even when the would-be hero dies at the end, then . . . we still got to see them fight, didn't we? We still learned how we ourselves might fight, when pressed? And, if that hero dies, if the horror of the day wins, that's not even really sad, is it? When the horror wins, then that confirms certain things for us. It lets us understand our world and our reality that much better. It lets us slit our eyes harder against it, and be ready when it comes for us.

Because it can provoke a visceral response. A *physical* response. Have you ever been walking through a hotel lobby or a bus station and seen someone on a bench, lost in a horror novel? Sit down, watch them read. I mean—don't be a creeper, don't completely invade their privacy or make them choose a different bench. But watch the way, when they get to a certain part of the book, they maybe pull their feet up onto the bench. See how they keep licking their lips from nervousness, from tension. Listen for their heart beating harder. Is that a sheen of sweat on their face? It is. But they're sort of smiling too, aren't they? Of all the genres and modes of story out there, only two can actually make a person's blood pressure change, I think: erotica and horror. The rest have wonderful things they can impart, a lot of them spark great and necessary conversations, some make you feel less alone, some let you check out of your reality for a few hundred pages or a couple hours, and that's wonderful—thank you, other genres. We need all of that, and more. But we also need our blood pressure to spike, just from words on a page. I forever love that horror can do this not to us, but *for* us.

Because of the chuckles. Jokes and humor in horror, they're pressure release valves. Without the funny stuff, then horror climbs up to that shrieky plateau and just stays there, flatlining at a steady scream, and . . . without variation, without that up-down unpredictable rhythm of engaging storytelling, then the reader loses interest. Yes, they're there for the horror, for the blood, for the terror, for the spooky stuff, but the humor is the other side of that eternally spinning coin. It's hard to pull off scares without some laughs sprinkled in. And it doesn't have to be setup/punch-line jokes, it doesn't have to be slapstick—it can be the smallest little asides, the blackest of sick humor. And, often, it should be that, as laughter rings hollow in a tomb. In the swirling nightmare horror can be, though, even the slightest little crack of a grin, that can be monumental—and I'll never not be in love with that.

Because there are real and actual scary things. Yes, horror's a roller coaster with the safety bar down: the reader gets to plunge and climb and loop and scream, experience all the rush, but . . . all with the assurance that they're not going to go flying off into open space, come down a jagged, broken wreck. We need those rides. However. There's horror you *don't* engage, isn't there? Novels, films, poems, sculptures, video games, paintings, songs, cosplay, stage plays, television, comic books, videos online, animation, whatever—we've all been around this merry-go-round enough times to have a kind of sense of what might be dangerous for us to engage, don't we? Our own personal barometers meant to keep us safe? Ask yourself why you avoid this or that, I'm saying. I think it's because we all know that art not only *can* change you, but it's *supposed* to. Horror's art. You experience it, and you come out the other side a different person. However, with some of this transgressive stuff you're letting in, there's no guarantee you're coming out a better person, is there? This story element, that imagery, it might open a door inside you that you didn't even know you were keeping shut. And that's truly scary. Horror, it's got fun teeth, sure. But it's also got some real teeth, if you reach your arm in deep enough. And? Sometimes even when you don't. That danger, it makes horror fun, doesn't it? You don't know for sure that you're coming out the other side the same person you were when you paid at the gate. It can be a dangerous game, yes—not all the safety bars come down on this particular ride. But we all line up for it again and again.

Because it's been there for me when I needed it. Like somebody I know once said, horror's not a symptom, it's a love affair. I feel like horror's saved me over and over. So, getting to be the big evil chicken with a pen in his beak, that's the highest honor. Not because I stand among giants, but because I'm standing on the same floor as every one of my readers. We're a sea of black T-shirts, we've all got tickets in our hands, and we don't know if we're going to scream or laugh this time out—probably both— but we can't stop now, can we? And anyway, we like the people lined up with us here. We see ourselves in each other, and we help each other stand taller, and, sure, we might end up puking in the aisle from what we see, we might have to leave the light on at bedtime, but when we scream and clutch each other's arms, that's when we're the most human. That's when we're the most ourselves. So we put some ketchup on our hot dog, and if some of it gets on our shirt, so what? We're all friends here. And anyway, if it looks like blood, that's all the better, isn't it?

Stay golden terrified,
Stephen Graham Jones
Boulder, CO
18 April 2024

About the Authors

Clay McLeod Chapman writes books, comic books, and YA/middle grade books, as well as for film and television. His most recent novel is *Wake Up and Open Your Eyes*.

David Demchuk is the award-winning author of *The Bone Mother* and *RED X*. His third novel, *The Butcher's Daughter*, cowritten with debut author Corinne Leigh Clark, was published in 2025 by Soho Press (US) and Titan Books (UK). Born and raised on the Canadian prairie, David now lives in a house by the sea with his husband and Labrador in St. John's, Newfoundland.

Tananarive Due is an American Book Award and NAACP Image Award–winning author, who was an executive producer on *Horror Noire: A History of Black Horror* for Shudder and teaches Afrofuturism and Black Horror at UCLA. She and her husband, science fiction author Steven Barnes, cowrote the graphic novel *The Keeper* and an episode for Season 2 of *The Twilight Zone* for Paramount+ and Monkeypaw Productions. Due is the author of several novels and two short story collections,

Ghost Summer: Stories and *The Wishing Pool and Other Stories.* She is also coauthor of a civil rights memoir, *Freedom in the Family: A Mother-Daughter Memoir of the Fight for Civil Rights* (with her late mother, Patricia Stephens Due). Learn more at TananariveDue.com.

Rachel Harrison is the *USA Today* bestselling author of *Play Nice, So Thirsty, Black Sheep, Such Sharp Teeth, Cackle,* and *The Return,* which was nominated for a Bram Stoker Award for Superior Achievement in a First Novel. Her short fiction has appeared in *Guernica,* in *Electric Literature*'s Recommended Reading, as an Audible Original, and in her story collection *Bad Dolls.*

Sadie Hartmann, aka Mother Horror, is the co-owner of the monthly horror fiction subscription company Night Worms and the Bram Stoker Award–winning author of *101 Horror Books to Read Before You're Murdered* from Page Street Publishing. Her second book, *Feral & Hysterical: Mother Horror's Ultimate Reading Guide to Dark and Disturbing Fiction,* will be released in August 2025. She lives in the Pacific Northwest with her husband of twenty-plus years, where they stare at Mount Rainier, eat street tacos, and hang out with their three kids.

Grady Hendrix is a *New York Times* bestselling novelist and screenwriter who owns too many paperbacks and not enough shelves. He's the author of *Witchcraft for Wayward Girls, How to Sell a Haunted House, The Final Girl Support Group, The Southern Book Club's Guide to Slaying Vampires,* and many more, including *Paperbacks from Hell,* a history of the horror paperback boom of the '70s and '80s that won the Bram Stoker Award for Superior Achievement in Nonfiction. (All those paperbacks are for "research" and he needs them.) His books have sold over two million copies and have been translated into more than twenty languages. He lives in New York City and will die there, too, probably crushed to death beneath piles of paperbacks. Learn more useless facts about him at www.gradyhendrix.com.

Gabino Iglesias is the author of the Shirley Jackson Award– and Bram Stoker Award–winning novel *The Devil Takes You Home*, as well as the critically acclaimed and award-winning novels *Zero Saints*, *Coyote Songs*, and *A House of Bone and Rain*. He is a writer, journalist, professor, and literary critic living in Austin, Texas. He is the horror columnist for *The New York Times Book Review*.

Stephen Graham Jones is the *New York Times* bestselling author of *The Only Good Indians*, *My Heart Is a Chain Saw*, and *I Was a Teenage Slasher*. He has been an NEA Literature Fellowship recipient and a recipient of several awards, including the Ray Bradbury Prize from the *Los Angeles Times*, the Bram Stoker Award, the Shirley Jackson Award, the Jesse H. Jones Award for Best Book of Fiction from the Texas Institute of Letters, the Independent Publisher Book Award for Multicultural Fiction, and the Alex Award from the American Library Association. He is the Ivena Baldwin Professor of English at the University of Colorado Boulder.

Alma Katsu is the award-winning author of eight novels, including *The Hunger* ("supernatural suspense at its finest" —*The New York Times*) and, most recently, *The Fervor* ("a feat of pure storytelling" —*The New York Times*). Her books have won or been nominated for the Bram Stoker, Locus, Goodreads, and Shirley Jackson awards and made best books lists with NPR, *Library Journal*, Oprah, Barnes & Noble, Amazon, and more. Her next novel, *Fiend* (coming September 2025), has been optioned for a TV series.

Brian Keene is the author of more than fifty books, three hundred short stories, and dozens of comic books and graphic novels. His work has been translated into over a dozen languages and has won numerous literary awards. Several of his books and stories have been adapted for film. In addition to writing, Keene was the showrunner for Realm Media and BlackBoxTV's *Silverwood: The Door* and has served as a producer or executive producer on several feature films, including the award-winning *I'm Dreaming of a White Doomsday* and *Dead Format*. From 2015 to 2020, he hosted the immensely popular *The Horror Show with Brian Keene* podcast, which returned to the airwaves in 2025. He also serves on the board of directors for the Scares That Care 501(c)(3) charity organization. The father of two sons and stepfather to one daughter, Keene lives in Pennsylvania with his wife, the author Mary SanGiovanni, and several cats.

John Langan is the author of two novels and six collections of stories. For his work, he has received the Bram Stoker and This Is Horror Awards. He is one of the founders of the Shirley Jackson Awards, for which he continues to serve on the board of advisors. He lives in New York's mid-Hudson Valley with his wife and younger son and on a clear day can see the Catskills.

Victor LaValle is the author of six previous works of fiction: three novels, two novellas, and a collection of short stories. His novels have been included in best-of-the-year lists by *The New York Times Book Review*, the *Los Angeles Times*, *The Washington Post*, *Chicago Tribune*, *The Nation*, and *Publishers Weekly*, among others. He has been the recipient of a Guggenheim Fellowship, an American Book Award, the Shirley Jackson Award, and the Key to Southeast Queens. He lives in New York City with his wife and kids and teaches at Columbia University.

Josh Malerman is a *New York Times* bestselling author and one of two singer-songwriters for the rock band the High Strung. His debut novel, *Bird Box*, is the inspiration for the hit Netflix film of the same name. His other novels include *Unbury Carol*, *Inspection*, *A House at the Bottom of a Lake*, *Pearl*, *Goblin*, *Daphne*, *Incidents Around the House*, and *Malorie*, the sequel to *Bird Box*. Malerman lives in Michigan with his fiancée, the artist-musician Allison Laakko.

Jennifer McMahon is the *New York Times* bestselling author of twelve suspense novels, including *The Winter People*, *Promise Not to Tell*, and *My Darling Girl*. She's written about ghosts, serial killers, shape-shifting monsters, an evil fairy king, a kidnapping rabbit, a terrifying swimming pool, and more. She lives on the Gulf Coast of Florida with her partner, Drea. When not writing, she spends a lot of time exploring and seeking out haunted places, real and imagined.

Nuzo Onoh is an award-winning writer of Igbo descent. Hailed as the Queen of African Horror, she is a pioneer of the African horror literary genre. Nuzo's works have been featured in numerous magazines, academic studies, and anthologies. She has given talks and lectures about African horror, including at the prestigious Miskatonic Institute of

Horror Studies, London. She has also appeared on many radio shows and podcasts, including BBC Radio 4's *Woman's Hour* and BBC World Service. Her works have been longlisted and shortlisted, and she is a Bram Stoker Lifetime Achievement Award recipient. Nuzo holds a law degree and master's degree in writing, both from the University of Warwick, England. She is a certified civil funeral celebrant, licensed to conduct nonreligious burial services. An avid musician with an addiction to Jungyup and K-indie, Nuzo plays both the guitar and piano and holds an NVQ in digital music production. She resides in the West Midlands, United Kingdom.

Cynthia Pelayo is a Bram Stoker Award and International Latino Book Award–winning author and poet. Her novels include *Vanishing Daughters*, *Forgotten Sisters*, *Children of Chicago*, and *The Shoemaker's Magician*. In addition to writing genre-blending novels that incorporate elements of fairy tales, mystery, detective, crime, and horror, Pelayo has written numerous short stories, the poetry collection *Crime Scene*, the story collection *Lotería*, and is the editor of the upcoming *Ghosts of Where We Are From*. She holds a master of fine arts in writing from the School of the Art Institute of Chicago. She lives in Chicago with her family. For more information, visit www.cinapelayo.com.

Hailey Piper is the Bram Stoker Award–winning author of *Queen of Teeth*, *All the Hearts You Eat*, *A Light Most Hateful*, *Teenage Girls Can Be Demons*, and other books of horror, including her newest novel, *A Game in Yellow*. She is the author of more than one hundred short stories appearing in *Weird Tales*, *PseudoPod*, *The End of the World as We Know It: New Tales of Stephen King's* The Stand, and other publications. She lives with her wife in Maryland, where their cosmic rituals are secret. Find Hailey at www.haileypiper.com.

Mary SanGiovanni is an award-winning American horror and thriller writer of nearly two dozen novels and novellas, including her most recent media tie-in novel for the *Alien* franchise, *Enemy of My Enemy*; her fan-favorite Kathy Ryan series; and *For Emmy*, soon to be made into a film. She has also written short stories, comics for Marvel and DC, and nonfiction. Her work has been translated internationally. She has a master's degree in writing popular fiction from Seton Hill University outside of Pittsburgh. She has the distinction of being one of the first women to speak about writing at the CIA headquarters in Langley, Virginia, and offers talks and workshops around the country on writing. Born and raised in New Jersey, she currently resides in Pennsylvania.

Paul Tremblay has won the Bram Stoker, British Fantasy, Sheridan Le Fanu, and Massachusetts Book Awards and is the *New York Times* bestselling author of *Horror Movie*, *The Beast You Are*, *The Pallbearers Club*, *Survivor Song*, *Growing Things and Other Stories*, *Disappearance at Devil's Rock*, *A Head Full of Ghosts*, and the crime novels *The Little Sleep* and *No Sleep Till Wonderland*. His novel *The Cabin at the End of the World* was adapted into the Universal Pictures film *Knock at the Cabin*. His essays and short fiction have appeared in *The New York Times*, *The Boston Globe*, the *Los Angeles Times*, and numerous "year's best" anthologies. He lives outside of Boston, Massachusetts, with his family and has a master's degree in mathematics.

Acknowledgments

Why I Love Horror began as an idea for my library training blog, but in the decade-plus since it began, until today—with you reading this book—I was never alone.

First I need to thank the eighteen authors and one illustrator who agreed to participate in this venture. Every single one of them said yes, immediately, when I asked them to be a part of this project. At that point all I had was an idea. We had no book deal, no timeline, nothing. Their trust in me will always be humbling. Brian Keene, Hailey Piper, John Langan, Alma Katsu, Gabino Iglesias, Tananarive Due, Jennifer McMahon, Josh Malerman, Paul and Emma Tremblay, Grady Hendrix, Cynthia Pelayo, Clay McLeod Chapman, Nuzo Onoh, Rachel Harrison, Victor LaValle, Mary SanGiovanni, David Demchuk, and Stephen Graham Jones—I am so proud of what we have done together.

However, a special note of deep gratitude goes always and forever to Brian Keene. Everything I have done in relation to horror goes back to the early days of this century, when, as Brian's professional life was falling apart, he took the time to answer an email from a baby librarian asking for more information about the collapse of the horror paperback market.

He did not have to answer that email. But not only did he take the time to explain everything to me, he has also stayed in my corner from that day forward. He was literally there for me when no one else was. As I attended my first StokerCon, knowing no one, he held my hand virtually from the other side of the country, encouraging me to text him at all hours if I had questions, and he answered! He also contacted people he knew (without telling me) to make sure I felt welcome and safe. And that is but one example from almost twenty years of friendship. Everything I have accomplished in this genre stands on the foundation of encouragement that Brian laid down for me.

And a special shout-out to Cynthia and the entire Pelayo family. I treasure the very real friendship our families have forged over the last handful of years. And to think, without your books, we never would have met.

Speaking of Cynthia, she brought Lane Heymont into my life. When I decided that I wanted to make *Why I Love Horror* into a book, I asked Cynthia if she thought Lane would want to talk about it. Not only did he say yes, but he has also been my biggest cheerleader since that first phone call. Thanks to everyone at the Tobias Literary Agency who has helped Lane help me. I am so lucky and proud to be a part of "Team Lane."

Joe Monti and Caroline Tew at Saga did the heavy lifting on making this physical book you have just read, including contacting Jeffrey Alan Love, who provided the amazing cover art. I also want to thank Melissa Croce, Karintha Parker, and Savannah Breckenridge for their tireless work making sure libraries and readers knew about this book. But back to Joe: we have known each other for years, but it was always as you, the editor, and me, the reviewer. Both of us working from different perches, but always with the same goal—to get horror into more readers' hands.

When Lane reached out to you about this book, you were on board immediately. I am honored by the faith you had in adding me to your amazing stable of Saga authors. I can't wait to see what we can accomplish now that we are officially working together.

Sadie Hartmann, what began as me mentoring you has become a treasured friendship. We are two women forging our own paths through this genre, but always together in our support of each other. Thank you for providing the introduction here even when you were swamped finishing your own book.

There are a few authors who were almost in this book. Some had to be cut, others declined because of other commitments. Thank you to Gwendolyn Kiste, Silvia Moreno-Garcia, Cassandra Khaw, Catriona Ward, Eric LaRocca, Tim McGregor, Lee Murray, Tobi Ogundiran, and Premee Mohamed.

Ellen Datlow provided me essential advice in the business of editing an anthology. From sharing her contract language to behind-the-scenes accounting tips and more, this book would not have happened without her. And much thanks to my dear friend and colleague Karen Toonen for her help taking Ellen's documentation and making my version of it.

To my editors, past and present: Susan Maguire at *Booklist* and Melissa DeWild, Stephanie Klose, and Kiera Parrott at *Library Journal*, thank you for wrangling my words all year long, even though I often curse your measly 170-to-200-word limit, but (and you won't catch me admitting this ever again) that word limit and your expertise have made me a stronger writer over the last ten years.

Thank you to everyone at ALA Editions, the publishers of my first three books, but especially Jamie Santoro, Rob Christopher, and Ramon Robinson.

There are many people who have supported me in ways that need official thanking. I have expressed my appreciation to them all in person over the years, but the world needs to know how important these people are to me: Daniel Kraus, Stephanie Sendaula, Robin Bradford, Stephen Sposato, Ashley Rayner, Maxwell Gold, Brian Matthews, Linda Addison, Meghan Arcuri, John Palisano, John Edward Lawson, Lisa Kröger, Jim Chambers, Lisa Wood, Angela Yuriko-Smith, Kelly Jensen, Carolyn Ciesla, Julia Smith, Cyndi Robinson, John Rehor, Michael Allen Rose, Ben Rubin, Meghan Bouffard, Emily Hughes, JG Faherty, Jocelyn Codner, Lisa Morton, Greg Greene, Robb Olson, Christopher Hawkins, Shawnna Deresch, Damian Serbu, John Everson, Brian Pinkerton, Lisa Quigley, Mackenzie Kiera, Stephanie Gagnon, Kristi Chadwick, Alex Brown, Misha Stone, Steve Thomas, Joyce Saricks, Neal Wyatt, Joyce Hagen-McIntosh, Katie Gardner, Becky Sorice, Andrea Hernandez, Fran Hurt, Margaret and Bill Coffee, Nancy and John Kent, Jody and Kevin Cahill, Jim and Diane Danbury, Paul and Lois Hummel, and everyone who I have served with or encountered through my work with the Horror Writers Association.

To Emily Vinci, Konrad Stump, Lila Denning, and Yaika Sabat. Dedicating the book to you was a no-brainer. Our real-life friendship is precious to me, but our group chat is everything. Together we have made being a "Halloween Librarian" a thing, and along the way we have been there supporting each other through some truly difficult times and celebrating each other in the happiest of moments as well.

Before the Halloween Library League, though, there was, and still is, my library ride or dies: Rebecca Vnuk and Magan Szwarek. I love you both.

To the thousands of library workers who I have encountered, taught, met at a conference, inspired through something I wrote, and more: I see you all. I know how hard it is out there. I will continue to use my platform and voice to fight for us and the essential work we do, every day.

To Alyssa Miller, my best friend since I was fourteen. We have been through everything together. Thank you for always being there and, also, for allowing me to use you as an example in my training programs.

Family is very important to me, and I have a great one. Thanks to my sisters Amy and Emily, and sister-in-law Melanie. To my late in-laws, Mitch and Olesja Spratford, who, while no longer here, entered my life when I was a teenager, always loved and supported me, and are always in my heart. And to my parents, Linda and Robert Siegel, who never put limits on what I could read, dropped me off at the library and let me explore for hours (shout-out to the Hunterdon County Library in my hometown of Flemington, New Jersey), and set the example of prioritizing service to your community.

To my now grown children Sam and Nate. I am proud of the people you have become. You are kind, creative, and talented. Thanks for taking it to heart when you were little and I told you "normal is boring." I will be there to root you on as you pursue your dreams, just like you did for me. I love you with everything I have in me.

And finally, to my husband Eric, the love of my life and my best friend. We met when we were barely adults and have grown together through college and postgrad degrees, into our fourth decade. We have both risen to the top of our professions and raised two amazing children along the way, but it is the fact that we have done it hand in hand, as a team, for which I am most thankful. Your support has never wavered, and in fact, you often believe in me before I believe in myself. Going through this scary world is a lot easier with your love by my side.

Credits

About the Editor

Becky Siegel Spratford, MLIS, is a librarian specializing in serving patrons ages thirteen and up. She trains library staff all over the world on how to match books with readers through the local public library. She writes reviews for *Booklist* and a horror review column for *Library Journal*. Known for her work with horror readers, Becky is the author of three textbooks for library workers, most recently *The Readers' Advisory Guide to Horror* (3rd ed., ALA Editions, 2021). She is on the Shirley Jackson Award Advisory Board and is a proud member of the Horror Writers Association, currently serving as the association's secretary and cochair of its library committee. She lives with her husband just outside of Chicago, where they raised their now adult children.